DARKNESS DOES NOT COME AT ONCE

GLENN BRYANT

The Book Guild Ltd

First published in Great Britain in 2024 by
The Book Guild Ltd
Unit E2 Airfield Business Park,
Harrison Road, Market Harborough,
Leicestershire LE16 7UL
Tel: 0116 2792299
www.bookguild.co.uk
Email: info@bookguild.co.uk
X: @bookguild

Copyright © 2024 Glenn Bryant

The right of Glenn Bryant to be identified as the author of this
work has been asserted by them in accordance with the
Copyright, Design and Patents Act 1988.

All rights reserved. No part of this publication may be
reproduced, transmitted, or stored in a retrieval system, in any form or by any means,
without permission in writing from the publisher, nor be otherwise circulated in
any form of binding or cover other than that in which it is published and without
a similar condition being imposed on the subsequent purchaser.

This work is entirely fictitious and bears no resemblance to any persons living or dead.

Typeset in 11pt Minion Pro

Printed and bound by CPI Group (UK) Ltd, Croydon, CR0 4YY

ISBN 978 1916668 638

British Library Cataloguing in Publication Data.
A catalogue record for this book is available from the British Library.

For Juliet

I

Germany, 1939

Abbe and Meike felt far from home, standing a few paces away. Two police cars were parked close to where they both hesitated, at the bottom of the entrance to the thin drive leading up to their house. A winter's night wrapped around them like a shark. Abbe and Meike continued to pause their steps, wary of what awaited them. Beneath majestic trees, witnesses to time, they cast uneasy eyes at each other, and they shared an unconvincing smile. Abbe loved Meike so much.

There was no sign of any police officers in the sea of black, punctuated only by the outline of the approach to their home. The two of them began cautiously making their way up the driveway, Abbe steadfastly behind Meike, when figures turned torchlight sharply in their direction.

'Mr Steinmann? Mr Abbe Steinmann?' a voice called through blinding white.

'I am Abbe Steinmann.'

'May we go inside for a moment?' the man continued, becoming half visible.

'Yes... we may,' Abbe said, worried.

'What's going on?' said Meike, looking up from her wheelchair at Abbe, her voice creased with concern.

'Inside,' an officer said to her, 'please.'

Anxious, Abbe struggled to manoeuvre limp hands through jacket pockets in search of the keys to their house. He did not know what was happening and he instinctively feared the impending weight of life-changing news. The officers watched him unlock the front door before two of them pushed past him and began rifling through rooms. What were they doing, Abbe's eyes, written with panic, questioned? He tried not to look down at Meike.

'Mr Steinmann? You do know why we're here?' an officer said, but Abbe only looked back at him blank. 'Do you really want us to do this in front of your daughter?'

2

Abbe became unconscious of his actions, moving his feet forward one after the other, into a crowded corner of what until now had been a sanctuary, his family kitchen. A wall of officers separated him from Meike, who he did not dare look in the eye. He crouched his body down low into a ball, amid the tall bodies tightly surrounding him, and he proceeded to untie and then remove his shoes, as if he had happily arrived home from work one evening. *How ridiculous*, a voice in his head said, and yet his body had not known how else to respond.

'Mr Steinmann, you are arrested on suspicion of listening to foreign broadcasts by the British BBC.'

There it was, the terrifying statement which coldly reduced Abbe's existence to an apparition. He looked down at his hands in disbelief, as if they were so fragile they would pass through a wall were he to try and right himself.

'Dad… what's happening?' Meike cried, but Abbe had no answer, not for her, or for any of it. 'What's happening?' she cried.

3

At the police station, Abbe was being processed, turning his head down submissively and only glancing up to answer questions when they were put to him. A female official asked him to confirm his details and Abbe only had to mouth, 'Yes,' if he wished, in reply.

She asked him if he drank.

Occasionally.

Had he been drinking this evening?

Modestly.

Finally, she asked Abbe if he had ever contemplated taking his own life and Abbe's eyes widened in surprise, searching the police station floor like the answer lay there.

'Not really,' he said and the female official standing in front of him tightened her eyes. She leant forward and scribbled on a form, routinely asking Abbe to remove his shoes, his belt and his raincoat, which Abbe proceeded to blankly, but not before somehow feeling infected by the request. He soon realised what the woman was afraid of, what *they* were afraid of. He was being placed on suicide watch.

He was led away to a cell unsettlingly deep in the station, and he flinched when he walked past other cells harbouring disconnected voices, which seemed to belong to ghosts, not real Berliners Abbe might have once recognised. The officer leading him ignored their pleas, Abbe noticed.

As they walked, Abbe tried to hide his panic and calmly explained to the man that confined spaces did not agree with him, they never had, but his plea fell on cold ears. Meekly, as he had been ordered to do so, Abbe carried his shoes and attempted to accept the situation, his situation. *How had he got here?*

The man in front then stopped and asked Abbe to place his shoes outside of a cell door waiting ajar. As Abbe bent down to do so, he realised that every cell on the thin, metal corridor had a pair of shoes waiting vacant outside. *I don't belong here*, his instincts panicked.

Abbe entered the tight cell and horror rushed around him, like the moment a bad dream plummets like a rollercoaster, and yet Abbe couldn't wake now. He soothed the flat of one of his hands over his breast and he tried to control his breathing. He was going to be locked in here indefinitely. *He was going to be locked in here indefinitely.* This was his worst nightmare.

Abbe's instinct was to survey the cell he found himself in on fast forward. Grey, nothing notable, except to his right an old mattress lying flat on concrete and covered by a blanket, uncaring on top. He quickly experienced a drop in temperature before the door wheeled shut behind, surprising him. Abbe couldn't react before it locked heavily, followed by retreating footsteps he dare not consider carefully. He was all alone.

He rushed across the small cell and lay face down on the old mattress, so thin and so grim that it punishingly felt like part of the floor itself. He pulled the blanket, wiry in his fingers, over his head as if it was the only thing now separating him from madness. A light bulb, brighter than any July Abbe could remember growing up in Berlin, blinded his eyes from the centre of the ceiling. Its glare meant that there was little chance of sleep and escaping his confinement that way.

Defeated, Abbe opened his eyes and witnessed the light dulled by the blanket's material, which he continued to pull tight to his face. He closed his eyes once more and he thought of nothing, nothing. Everything was over, his life was over. His life.

Abbe thought that this was the moment that he would cry, that he would begin to break, before another inmate, incarcerated at the station, screamed out. The cry's echoes fingered every crack of concrete in the building with an ominous clarity. Nobody was coming, Abbe realised, as his frame once more locked into tension, listening out for any sound of hope.

Abbe pulled the blanket back tightly over his head and closed his eyes. All he could picture was black possibilities haunting his future like tarpaulin following a firefight, cloaking corpses in the dangerous breeze.

4

The door to Abbe's cell yawned open. Disturbed, he pulled the blanket from his face, and he began picking his long frame up off of the floor, unfolding himself into a standing position and steadying himself.

'May I use the lavatory?' he said, releasing a breath from his chest now that he could see the door to his cell was open.

'Of course,' said the officer who had come to collect him.

Abbe was led by the officer to a neighbouring cell, empty and with a hole in the floor in one corner. He could not quite believe what he was being invited to do and proceeded – medievally, he felt – to urinate into the hole in the floor while the officer waited for him to finish.

'May I have a glass of water?' Abbe said after turning back to face the man, while keeping his chin tucked in as he focused on buttoning the fly on his trousers. Abbe's current conscious shrugged at the indignity.

'Yes… yes,' the officer said.

Abbe was taken to another room, again antiseptic

and grey. A small table anchored its centre and was bookmarked by two chairs. A senior looking officer took a confident seat across from Abbe, who remained standing for a moment and, without looking up, the officer opened a blue folder and began reading from it. Preparations had been made, Abbe was disturbed to witness, and cautiously he took a seat opposite the official, as if the chair which had been left for him was balanced over a gallows. Abbe looked down briefly.

'Mr Steinmann, do you recognise this?' the officer opposite him said, showing him a photograph of a shortwave radio Abbe immediately did recognise. *Breathe*, his mind counselled.

'No... no, I don't,' Abbe said, and the officer frowned.

'Mr Steinmann, do you own an item like this?'

'No... no, I don't,' Abbe repeated.

Breathe, he willed himself and the officer changed tack, which Abbe was eternally grateful for.

'Your daughter... Meike, I believe,' he said, and Abbe instinctively disliked her name being spoken out loud, as if the man was putting his hands on her without permission. 'She gave my officers a message before they left your home tonight. She was insistent,' he said. 'She said that she loved you, and that she will still love you, whatever has happened... whatever you've done. Whatever you've done.'

Abbe closed his eyes and he breathed, blinking them back open. *Meike*. The simple mention of her was a reminder of a life he dare not invite here. Briefly, he pictured her kindness, and its memory warmed his shoulders like a blanket when the evening turns late in summer. Abbe then realised something. The police officers who had remained at his home tonight, manhandling its contents, had clearly not unearthed his shortwave radio, hidden, as he was now only achingly aware, in plain sight in his study. If they had not looked past it, they would have confronted him now with the discovery surely. *Surely.*

'Mr Steinmann, we are simply trying to get to the bottom of this,' the officer said. 'Surely you wish to clear this up?'

The officer's new tone helped slow Abbe's heart, but he continued to point his head downward in submission. His whole life might hang on his next few words.

'Mr Steinmann, have you ever owned an item like this?' the officer said, pointing with his eyes to a photograph he slowly snapped flat on the table between them.

Abbe paused and unlocked his hands.

'Mr Steinmann, this is a radio capable of listening to broadcasts by the British BBC… enemies of the Third Reich. Have you ever owned an item like this?'

The question hung between them.

'No,' Abbe said finally.

'You've never owned a radio like this?'

Abbe again paused. 'No,' he said.

5

Abbe, Meike and Anselma were sat, and were about to eat supper. Abbe and Meike were shaken from the previous evening and finding everything a challenge. Anselma, still oblivious, spent last night at her grandparents' and could only sense the depression weighing down their supper table already laden with plates and glasses.

Abbe had finally been released by police in the early hours of the morning, empty and alone. After arriving home and first visiting the bathroom, he immediately climbed into bed, fully clothed, as if he was forged from fine china, before Meike interrupted him, peeking into his room.

'Dad? Dad?' she said quietly.

'Meike?' he said, wary that she might be furious with him.

'Can I get into bed with you, Dad?' she said.

'Yes… yes, of course, sweetheart.'

She bumped open the door to her father's room with the front of her chair and wheeled in, anxious to embrace him. Abbe shifted in preparation to the far side of the bed, so that his daughter had room to transfer from her chair. In the darkness, she whispered gently to a count of three, 'One… two…' before making the hop from her wheelchair to the bed. Her head nodded gently in time as she did so. Through the dark, Abbe sensed his daughter's idiosyncrasies, his heart breaking. Following her accident, he couldn't remember a time when she had complained.

They hugged quickly before falling into a semblance of sleep, their body clocks painfully awaking them a few hours later. Sitting upright, Abbe looked down at his hands, shaking with shock. His head was a frightened whirlwind. *What on Earth should I do?*

One thing he had experienced upon returning home from the police station in the middle of the night, and despite not having eaten for twelve hours, was the most complete emptying of his bowels he could remember. *The strangest thing*, he had thought, climbing off their toilet like he was a thousand years old.

The three of them were sat now at their table in their dining room and Abbe looked up, first Meike and then at Anselma. A canyon separated the three of them. Meike was close to tears. Anselma began to eat hungrily as Abbe and her sister only mechanically forced thin mouthfuls between pursed lips. Anselma glanced across at both of them.

She said, 'Grandpa says this will turn into a second Great War soon. He believes Hitler will try to knock out France first before invading Britain… then Russia.'

Abbe looked at his eldest daughter and he held in a sigh. 'It will be a disaster for us all, Anselma,' he said, forcing the words out and Anselma was not sure how to respond.

'I have joined the local National Socialist Youth group,' she said.

'What?!'

'I have joined the National Socialist Youth, Father.'

'You've joined the Hitler Youth,' he said.

'It is my duty, Father... someone has to from this family.'

Meike smarted, but any anger she experienced only carried her closer to tears. Abbe looked into his youngest daughter's eyes, and he ached. He wanted to scream.

'There is no place in our Führer's Reich for people who are unproductive, Father. The Jews are holding us back...' Anselma said.

'Don't... use that language at this table,' Abbe said, eyes closed, which was all he could do to bottle his feelings.

'You should be happy that I am training to become a great mother... for Germany,' Anselma said.

'Training!' Abbe tutted. 'Use your mind, Anselma... your education... every word the National Socialists say—' But Abbe was cut off by Meike tugging gently on his arm. On the wireless, she had overheard the word "handicapped", which had caught her attention.

'Quiet... please, Father,' she said.

Oh, what now? Anselma's head complained as Abbe and Meike both turned their focus to the wireless sat above a fireplace on the far wall.

The broadcaster announced: 'All mentally and physically handicapped children, from the ages of sixteen to eighteen, must report as a priority to their local hospital or family physician. Nothing should detract German homes from the great effort in the struggle against our Jewish enemies.' The man on the wireless continued, 'While the rest of us are at war, the handicapped can live peacefully in specially designated centres, which will house the latest technology, and ensure after we are victorious that they are ready to rejoin and contribute to society.'

Silence. Abbe and Meike looked at one another, despair in their eyes. Meike was seventeen. Abbe tried a smile, but it was useless. *Please don't cry, my sweetheart*, his mind, aching from exhaustion, willed, *please don't*. But Meike's face crumpled into tears, her hands reaching up to hide her emotion as her breast heaved between sobs.

'Oh sweetheart...' Abbe said. 'Don't cry. Please don't cry,' he said softly, climbing from his chair at their table and wrapping his arms like wings around his daughter.

6

It was the following morning and Abbe felt himself at odds with the person he was previously. He knew the old him would have given in, accepted the inevitable, accepted what was "right", almost shaking his head in conversation with himself. Now, after the experience of the last few days, he regretted his old self.

'We have to move you, Meike,' he said, without lifting his eyes to look at his daughter, sat at their dining table, determined to have a decent breakfast. He reached across for their remaining butter left from last week's ration.

'Move me? Where, Father?' said Meike, wearing tired, puffy eyes.

'Somewhere… else,' he said. 'People know you are here. They also know now that you should report to the authorities. It only takes one person…' he said and paused, not allowing the idea to linger. Instead, Abbe busied himself spreading butter enthusiastically over bread and sipping steaming coffee from a mug, a day old and a little bitter, if he told himself the truth, but this morning still retaining a wonderful headiness. His senses were returning.

'If people no longer see you after today, that would be what they would expect,' he said before taking a bite of bread and butter, though he could now feel his stomach begin to tighten with tension.

'Are you sure, Father?' Meike said.

'Of course I'm sure, sweetheart.' He smiled and reached out a hand to her, but her fingers shrank back from the invitation. A sad half smile and Meike half-heartedly began eating a slice of bread and butter.

She closed her eyes. 'When will we move, Father? And where… to where?'

'Your grandparents' house,' Abbe said. 'And we are going tonight, Meike, tonight.'

Following breakfast, Meike pushed herself from their dining room through to her bedroom, on the ground floor of their home, bumping open the door to her room with the footrest of her chair. She gathered herself. She spied her suitcase sat open underneath her bedroom window. It was already half full as she was still to unpack it properly following a family holiday last summer. She hoiked it up and balanced it as best she could on her lap, pushing to her bed before roughly heaving the case onto it.

She looked about herself and began placing favourite items of clothing, books and toiletries into the suitcase, and then closing it. *Better*, she thought. She felt better for the first time since *it* had happened, her father's arrest in their home by the police.

Soon, darkness was close outside. Abbe could feel tension creeping up his body, like it had been secretly planted by the police throughout the floor of their home. You had to be careful where you stepped. He packed

Meike's things into their car, his senses remaining on high alert for any uncommon noise.

Inside, Meike pushed through to their kitchen with a final suitcase balanced on her lap. She entered as her father did so from outside and she tried to convince him with a smile, just as he did in reply. Neither of them were entirely successful, united in the fear which had found them. They each made a silent wish.

'Right, let's get your case in the car,' Abbe said, striding over to Meike to collect her last suitcase and carry it outside.

Walking to the car, Abbe's hearing picked up voices in the darkness, down their lane, instantly making his skin prickle with heat against the cold. He stood still and he listened through his pumping heart, desperate to confirm that their intention was benign.

Back inside their kitchen, Anselma watched any confidence drain from Meike's face the moment her father left them once more.

'Bye, Anselma,' Meike offered.

'Bye,' her sister said as their father, who wasn't sure if he was interrupting, returned.

'Are we ready?' he asked.

'Yes,' said Meike, fighting a fierce pull to stay.

'Okay,' said Abbe. 'Anselma… we won't be long. We'll just get your sister settled… then I shall be straight back. Don't wait up if you don't want to.'

'Okay.'

'Bye, Anselma,' Meike tried once more, hopefully, before finally following her father outside. She navigated the front door's lip in her chair, and she freewheeled down a short ramp her father had fitted following her accident before purposefully pushing the few yards to their car. She pulled ajar the open passenger door and she positioned herself in preparation for transferring to the front passenger seat.

Once Meike was safely inside the car, Abbe made his way around the vehicle and began dismantling her wheelchair, removing her seat cushion first and then folding the backrest down. He released both wheels, pushing them free from their centre and collapsing the chair completely, carefully lifting the individual parts onto the car's back seats.

It was dusty black in the driveway of their rural home, leading out onto the lane, which wound up like a stream to the junction of a larger road, heading south and into Berlin, or going north deeper into the countryside. It was a little after 10pm, reassuringly quiet. Perfect.

The car remained stationary, and Abbe and Meike shared a look and uncertain smiles before they both looked forward. Sat in the dark, the car's leather smelt cold. Abbe cranked the engine into life, and he carefully reversed out into their lane, flicking the car's headlamps on only once they were clear of their home. They reached the top of their lane, opening out onto the main road and wide enough now to take traffic in either direction. Abbe peered out from behind the steering wheel, and he looked left and right, before turning towards Berlin.

The road into the city and its outskirts was deserted until car headlamps intruded sharply behind them, making them both flinch like the police officers' flashlights, which had blinded them at the beginning of this nightmare.

Abbe instinctively did not like to speed, but now, looking across to Meike with alarm, he squeezed his right foot down on the car's accelerator and he surged the vehicle forward. The vehicle remained tight behind them as they entered Berlin's city limits. *Where was everyone?* Abbe's mind urged. He wanted witnesses, not isolation, now.

The car tailing them mercifully dived off down a sideroad and vanished as quickly as it had appeared. Abbe looked across to Meike and shared a half smile, real in relief now, though it felt best to maintain polite silence until they reached their destination. Neither of them was in any mood to tempt fate.

They soon entered a wealthy boulevard, tucked away from the hustle of the main roads into Berlin and home to Abbe's in-laws, Hans and Marta. Abbe eased off the gas and allowed the vehicle to taxi gently to a stop, pulling up on the side of the avenue. He almost forgot and then he quickly shut off the car's headlamps.

Inside their home, Meike's grandparents, Hans and Marta, were anxiously waiting. On seeing them pull up, Marta hurried outside to be met by Abbe climbing nervously from his car. He felt a hundred years old.

'Hi, Marta,' he said, kissing her quickly on the cheek.

'Hello, Abbe… Meike,' she greeted, leaning into the front of the vehicle through the open door.

'Hi!' Meike waved from inside.

'Go in, go in…' Abbe hushed. 'Let's not make a scene.'

'Yes, yes, of course…' Marta said. 'Sorry, Abbe… of course.'

The grand boulevard where Marta and Hans lived was asleep now. Proud trees stood guard outside rich homes.

Out of the corner of his eye, Abbe noticed debris lying out of place, discarded on the otherwise immaculate pavement, personal items and a suitcase fractured, exposing an expensive claret blouse.

'Father, what is all that lying there?' Meike said, preparing to transfer into her chair.

'I don't know,' he lied, thinking it must be the result of hurried evictions he had heard of taking place, of a Jewish family. 'Let's not worry about that now... let's get you inside,' he said, busying himself unfolding the skeleton of her wheelchair and snapping it slowly back into full, standing position. From the centre of either spokes, Abbe pushed on the wheels one at a time, which was difficult in the dark.

'Less haste, Abbe,' he whispered to himself.

A padded seat completed her chair, ready for her to hop into. After transferring from the seat of the car, Meike held her body up a fraction to unfold a crease in her underwear. *Got it*, she thought before allowing her bottom to fall happily at full speed. Abbe unloaded the car's trunk and he carried Meike's suitcases inside as the light from Marta's hallway glared out onto the sidewalk, agitating his anxiety.

'Come... come, Meike,' he said. 'Inside... quickly.'

'Yes, Father,' she said, knowing now was not the time to test him.

Abbe bumped Meike in her chair up two steps to the front door of the home, which was awkward, because each step had to be tackled individually and, in his haste, Abbe jolted Meike in her chair and immediately winced. He hated hurting her.

'I'm sorry, sweetheart,' he whispered, leaning forward.

'Don't worry, Dad. It's okay,' she said, hiding her shock at the jolt.

Abbe took a breath and balanced his daughter and her chair up onto its back wheels carefully, so that he could roll her slowly over the final step. There. He let go, allowing her to take over and push in through the front door to the home, and his heart rate immediately began to drop.

'Right… I am going to go, sweetheart,' he called, seeing her safely inside. 'Goodnight, sweetheart… sleep well and I will be back soon. We can have supper one night!'

'Bye, Dad!' Meike beamed. 'Sleep well too!'

Abbe watched Marta close and lock the front door behind her and he allowed himself a moment. His daughter was safe. For now. He turned and let his footsteps fall down the steps back out onto the suburban street. At the bottom of them, he bumped into a woman, a Mrs Jaeger, who lived opposite, out walking her Alsatian before bedtime and the two of them considered each other momentarily.

'Good evening, Mr Steinmann,' Mrs Jaeger said, breaking the impasse first.

'Good evening, Mrs Jaeger. Nice to see you,' he said, eyes wide.

'You are late going home tonight,' she said before noticing Abbe had left the trunk of his car open. *Damn and blast*; he noticed, trying to hide his annoyance. He regathered himself.

'Yes, yes… a game of pontoon went on rather longer after supper than we had anticipated!'

'Was Meike with you earlier?' she tested, and Abbe's heartbeat quickened.

'No... no,' he said. 'Meike is always long in bed at this hour. Always been an early bird that one. She was born with the lark!' he jibed once more, and Mrs Jaeger smiled falsely. The pair of them exchanged eyes and agreed that it was time to end their dalliance.

'Well... it was nice seeing you, Mrs Jaeger,' he said. 'See you again, no doubt.'

'Good evening, Mr Steinmann,' she said, watching Abbe climb back into his car, where he grimaced, once she was safely out of view. *Blast*, he thought, *damn and blast*.

7

'Good morning, Meike!' Marta, her grandmother, said, walking into their dining room.

'Morning, Grandma,' said Meike, trying to smile.

'Coffee, Meike?' she asked.

'Of course she'll have coffee,' said her grandfather, Hans, grabbing a moment to enter the conversation. 'Good morning, Meike,' he added, then remembering his manners but more acutely remembering that Marta would scold him once they were alone if he had not.

'Good morning, Grandfather,' Meike said, warming up.

'Did you sleep well?' he asked.

'Not bad,' she said, and Hans nodded. Marta carefully walked over to their breakfast table and lovingly placed hot coffee and its steaming aroma in front of Meike.

'Oohhhh, thank you,' Meike said, wrapping her hands around the mug.

After breakfast, Meike wanted to go outside and get some air. At least the long boulevard her grandparents lived on was flat. She had pushed approximately 100 yards before taking a moment to sit still in her chair and enjoy the gentle February sun on her face, which she tilted skywards to catch as much as possible. A boy across the street noticed her. He had not seen her before and he could not help but stare blankly, like his mind was struggling to process her attraction into something he more easily understood.

Meike noticed him from the corner of her eye, with a wry smile in his direction, which surprised him. In the boy's experience, pretty girls always looked through him, he remembered with a regret older than his fifteen years. Meike refreshed her smile and raised her voice, so it carried across the street.

'Hello,' she said.

'Hello…' the boy said before Meike began pushing purposefully towards him, careful first to negotiate the kerb down to the road and then the step back up to the pavement upon reaching the other side. She knew that, unaided, both manoeuvres were difficult.

'I'm Meike,' she said, smiling beneath him. 'My grandparents live just back there,' and she motioned behind from where they were.

The boy's focus did not move from her, she noticed with a growing smile.

'I am staying with my grandparents for a while,' Meike said, and then she realised, with horror, her mistake, and immediately thought of her father and how upset he would be with her. Her demeanour changed. 'I shouldn't be out here… my father will be angry…' Her panic tumbled out, the boy realising. Nearly every family in Germany gathered each evening around the wireless to listen to the Party broadcast. It paid to.

'I like your grandparents' house,' he said and Meike was surprised by the mature manner of his reply, at odds with his teenage shyness. She couldn't put the two together in the moment.

'I live opposite you,' the boy said. 'Mr and Mrs Reis'... my parents.'

Meike nodded, but she was still struck by his previous words.

'I have to go,' he said. 'Errands for my mother... getting things we are missing in the pantry. I don't know if the shops will have everything, you know... these days. My mother finds it difficult to go out.'

'Yes,' said Meike. 'I understand... bye,' she said as the boy backed away, still facing her as he prepared to turn the corner of the boulevard.

'Bye,' the boy said, smiling.

I don't even know your name, Meike thought.

8

Days followed and the boy could not prevent his imagination replaying each moment of his meeting with Meike. The first smile, which he failed to return. Her second smile. The surprising 'Hello,' or had it been simply 'Hi?' His head was already clouding the perfection of each moment. That burst of purpose. *Yes.* To cross the road to see him, *him*. He couldn't ever remember a girl doing that for him before.

Eternal days turned into never-ending weeks, without so much of a glimpse of her, something to draw a new daydream from. The snapshots of Meike in Alfred's mind quickly became less and less clear, he realised, more and more fuzzy, only a blurring now of her beauty. The magic in her eyes. Her petite nose. Alfred felt fortunate in bed at night if her face returned to him crystal clear. But always fleetingly. He could never quite recall it again once he woke with a gasp. He had lost her all over again. He struggled to manage the emotions Meike was unlocking in him as he walked to school spellbound each day, glancing down at his scuffed school shoes, which he knew would trigger frustration in his mother, another schoolyard football match gotten out of hand. *How many times, Alfred?*

It was evening and Meike and her grandparents Marta and Hans were sat down and about to start eating their supper. Anselma was with them, but Abbe was not, leaving only an emptiness aching between them. They didn't know where he was.

He had been rearrested the previous evening. Anselma had been home when police officers had knocked on the door of their house. But no blind terror this time, only a knotted dread when Abbe had first opened his home to them. Abbe had quickly experienced a silent shaking in his body, but was it now finally calmed by relief, his head had questioned?

Every knock at their door. Every car pulling up, and loudly opening and closing doors down their lane. Telltale footsteps pacing up the gravel drive to their home. Following his first arrest, they each had tortured Abbe. Now that the same police officers' faces had returned, they did not look evil, Abbe had appreciated, stealing a furtive glance before reverting his eyes submissively to the floor holding him upright. The same officers were only malignant in their mission, Abbe's thoughts had concluded, as he felt no flush of heat, only the coldness of defeat.

'I'll get my shoes,' he said.

Meike and Anselma tried to turn their thoughts now back to their supper beneath them. The weight of lifting a spoon, leaden in their light hand, was heavy. Meike could feel her heart ache for her father, and she looked across to her sister, who she was grateful was mirroring her distress.

Meike's eyes returned to her bowl of vegetable soup before her. She tried to lift her spoon and fill it with the thin liquid and slim chunks of food, but it only weighed heavier each time she sank it deeper down into the bowl. Her stomach was pregnant with panic. Her father. How would he survive? How would she survive now without him?

Only last week, Meike had slurped her grandmother's vegetable soup down greedily with a guilty grin, catching her grandmother's eyes, happily watching her, as she ate and finally finished. Marta now looked down at her own bowl and the depression she felt weighed with regret at being too indulgent preparing the soup for supper earlier this afternoon. She had crammed too much veg in, vegetables she should have been saving sensibly for suppers later for the four of them this week. But she had wanted this evening to please the girls, her girls now, give them a little happiness back. Had that been asking too much?

Without Abbe as an anchor in her life, Marta felt frightened. What were she and Hans going to do?

Meike glanced across at her big sister, who instinctively knew she was becoming upset. Meike choked out an opening sob, which made Anselma flinch, followed by tears, like the first hesitation of heavy rain, running down Meike's cheeks.

'My darling,' Marta said, springing from her seat and folding her arms around her. But the kindness only unhinged the last of Meike's defences, her face collapsing completely between her hands. 'Oh darling,' Marta said. 'It'll be alright… it will be… alright.'

Hans sat and watched, a forced witness to his family's pain at the modest dining table the four of them hopelessly shared. He cast his eyes at Anselma, and he forced a small smile as she sat as if rooted to her chair. Then the worst thing. Anselma began to cry too, softly at first before loud sobs heaved from her in a way Hans had not heard before.

With sharp eyes, Marta quickly directed Hans to comfort Anselma, and he immediately rose to his feet and held his eldest granddaughter, hesitantly at first before embracing the situation and wrapping his wingspan around her like a beautiful bird. Anselma liked how it felt, wrapped beneath her grandfather.

Marta and Hans made eye contact once more from where they both now stood, respectively comforting their two granddaughters. Marta shook her head at Hans, her face and eyes asking him, telling him everything he already feared. What were they going to do?

9

It was Sunday morning and Marta and Anselma were adding finishing touches to their outfits for church. Hans was going to remain at home with Meike, who was happy for once to share her own company. That suited Hans handsomely. Time too for himself, time to read his newspaper, time to take over rolling a cigarette. Or two.

'Okay, Meike?' he said cheerily from his armchair, but failing to look up from his tall newspaper.

'Fine, Grandpa,' she said. Hans smiled warmly.

At church, Marta was surprising herself. She was enjoying attending this morning's sermon with Anselma, who was glad herself to be out of the house. The pair of them were walking out of church following the service, returning small smiles to fellow congregation members as they politely went. Marta then spotted Mrs Jaeger and she immediately wished she hadn't.

'Heil Hitler,' the two women, across islands of conversations, mouthed at each other.

Marta and Anselma continued to patiently make their way down the church's central aisle, in the queue for the timeless doors, beckoning them back out into the world. The reverend stood on duty beside them, wishing people well for another week.

'Ah... Mrs Richter,' he said when it was finally Marta and Anselma's time to pass. 'So lovely to see you... and lovely to see you, Anselma, here with us this morning. I hope you can come back and see us again soon.'

Anselma began to smile but pulled back from anything more.

'No... Mr Richter today?' the reverend asked.

'No, Reverend. Hans has been under the weather these past few days. He's enjoying catching up on his newspaper this morning.'

'I am sorry to hear that. Please pass on my best.'

'Yes... of course, Reverend,' Marta said and following final shared smiles, she and Anselma walked out into the fresh air and the peaceful church grounds. Marta looked up. The sky was grey and heavy overhead, bar blisters of white where sunlight was trying to break through. Something momentarily fluttered overhead before, just as fleetingly, becoming lost in the blanket above. *My eyes must have been playing a trick*, Marta thought.

Anselma then flinched as, in front of her, a piece of paper fell to earth. Strange. Where had it come from? What was it? Another piece of paper followed, floating gently down to earth, followed by another and another, and soon, more, much more.

Marta and Anselma, in unison, it seemed, with all members of this morning's congregation, looked up to the sky and witnessed thousands of pieces of white falling magically down through the grey like snow.

The pieces of paper soon formed a white carpet beneath their feet, peppered with black ink neither Marta nor Anselma could make out from where they stood. Marta stooped down to inspect the pieces of paper before being startled and quickly looking back up from her crouching position.

'Reverend... Reverend!' Mrs Jaeger said, instantly irritating Marta, who contained her contempt. 'Come quickly!'

'Yes, Mrs Jaeger?'

Everyone watched as the reverend hustled outside to witness for himself the covering of white on the ground. Odd pieces of paper continued to flap in the wind and Anselma caught one of them before it was able to fall to the floor and began reading from it before Marta had a chance herself.

Anselma read:

WARNING! WARNING!
Your rulers have condemned you to the massacres, miseries and privations of a war they can never hope to win.
They are lying to you: handicapped children you have loved are not being cared for by your government.
They instead are being experimented upon, tortured and starved. National Socialism does not harbour humanity enough to deem your children worthy of life. Stop supporting the German war effort immediately!

Silence for a moment between them before Marta made stern eyes at Anselma, who did not know what to think, flipping the small sheet over in her hand to reveal an inked stamp on the reverse side advertising the British Royal Air Force, the message's author, and Anselma immediately dropped it to the pavement as if she had been scolded.

'Let's get home,' Marta said, placing a hand on Anselma's arm and failing to conceal her concern through a smile. She was afraid that the Party's brown shirts would be here soon, as she discreetly pushed a crumpled copy of the British Air Force's flyer in her coat pocket. 'Come, Anselma,' she said.

'Heil Hitler, Mrs Richter,' Mrs Jaeger said, suddenly blocking her path.

'Heil Hitler, Mrs Jaeger,' said Marta, swallowing a curse.

'You don't believe any of this nonsense… do you, Mrs Richter? I mean, from the blasted British of all people?' she said.

'No…' said Marta. 'No,' she repeated more assured. 'I am as incensed as the rest of us… but I must get home to Hans, Mr Richter, he will calm me, Mrs Jaeger.'

'I do hope you are right, Mrs Richter. We must set the very best example to young Anselma here. Their generation must understand how stupid… how grasping these Jews are.'

Marta couldn't concentrate wholly on the conversation and Mrs Jaeger allowed the lack of an answer and smiled. 'Do pass on my regards,' she said, 'to Meike, when you next see her, which can never be long at the moment.'

Marta's blood ran cold. Mrs Jaeger could not possibly know. *How could she? Know?* And her of all people. Marta's mind spooled on fast forward, out of control, like a German fighter plane being chased to the ground by a trail of smoke. Marta always had to flinch away in that final moment, the sound of the impact making her insides jump.

10

Marta walked through the front door of their home and Hans immediately noticed her eyes – the panic. He let her be for a moment as she unbuckled her coat, fighting sniffs from her nose after walking energetically home. She hurried past Hans and clumsily filled a kettle full of water before slamming it down on the stove to boil.

'Marta... slow down, please,' Hans said. 'What *is* the matter?'

'Meike! Meike, come through, dear, come through,' Marta called, ignoring Hans for the moment. Meike was immediately worried. 'My dear... my dear,' she said, folding to her knees when she saw Meike push into their kitchen.

Hans spectated uneasily. 'Marta... do not scare the child,' he said.

'Does anyone know you are staying here?' Marta asked Meike, with frightened eyes, which only unseated Meike more.

'No, Grandmother... no,' she said before the thought flashed in her head. The boy across the street. *Oh no*, she realised. *Oh no*. 'I did go outside, Grandma, yes,' she said.

'Once... the following day, after arriving. I know it was wrong... I didn't realise... I know now, Grandma. I know.'

Anselma looked on.

'Marta, did something happen... at church?' said Hans, but Marta continued only to crouch claustrophobically in front of Meike, who was almost leaning back from her. 'Marta! What happened?' Hans said.

'This,' she said simply, finally climbing to her feet and turning to acknowledge her husband. She reached inside her coat pocket for the crumpled copy of the flyer.

'Grandmother!' Anselma said, upset to see it again. Hans looked past her reaction so that he could focus on the immediate task at hand, accepting the flyer from Marta and pushing his reading glasses up his nose as he did so in preparation. He began to read.

WARNING! WARNING!

[...]

National Socialism does not harbour the humanity to deem your children worthy of life. Stop supporting the German war effort immediately!

Hans finished reading and removed his spectacles. He paused, his eyes falling kindly on Meike first. He smiled lovingly at her.

'Your grandmother may be right, Meike,' he said. 'We may want to take this as a warning.'

'May?!' said Marta, instantly drawing sharp eyes from her husband.

He tried again to calm the discussion. 'It *may* be propaganda, but we all know what happened to your fa…' he said, checking himself at the last moment. 'There are very real dangers of being arrested now in Germany. Hitler and the government are taking anyone they want… and they will throw away the key…'

Marta now blew her eyes up even more wildly at Hans, who immediately closed his and realised his error. He opened his eyes again and looked at Meike, but it was too late. They both knew what each other was thinking and Meike's face buckled into tears, and Hans's heart broke.

'I'm so sorry, sweetheart… I didn't mean…' he said, reaching out a hand, left hanging in the air between them.

'Your grandfather didn't mean to sound so dramatic,' Marta said, crouching back down to hold the tops of Meike's arms, only interrupting her focus to turn her head around and shoot piercing eyes at Hans, stood helpless, looking down at the pair of them once more. Marta's attention was troubled by Anselma, stood expressionless, watching on, and she made a mental note.

Then, a knock at their door and everyone paused.

'Anselma… go and see who it is, please,' Marta said and Anselma walked out of the room in the direction of their door before returning.

'There is a boy,' she said. 'Asking for Meike. I think he lives across the street. Shall I ask him in?'

'No… no,' said Marta, struggling to look directly at her.

'Okay,' said Anselma, turning away and about to head back to their front door, which had been left ajar.

'No, don't,' Meike said, stopping her sister in her tracks. 'Send him through… please… to my room. Just give me a minute, to...' she said before beginning to push in that direction.

'Meike,' her grandmother said.

'Grandma, I'm fine,' she said, without turning around. 'I'm fine,' she said again, leaving Marta and Hans alone finally.

'Who is the boy?' Marta hissed at Hans.

'I don't know!' he said.

At the front door to their home, Anselma invited the boy from across the street in, pointing him curtly in the direction of her sister's room. He was unsure what to make of Anselma's manner before any disappointment he felt was quickly eclipsed by his excitement at seeing Meike again. Anselma pointedly looked at him as he walked politely past her, waiting for permission almost to proceed unescorted into their house. After a moment, Alfred began walking.

Looking down, each footstep he slowly placed forward prickled with his senses. Rich, red carpet underfoot. Decadent hangings on the wall. A smell different to his own parents' home. His heart thumped. He neared the end of the hallway. The door to Meike's room. Oh my God.

'Hi... come in,' Meike called after Alfred politely knocked on her room door.

'Hello,' Alfred said from behind it, opening it slowly.

'Hi,' Meike said, and Alfred took the sight of her in, like she was the night sky. *Say something, Alfred*, his mind then nudged him out of his trance.

'Hi... I am Alfred, from across the street. We met and spoke a few weeks ago,' he said, realising he sounded like a newspaper reporter, faithfully relaying the facts to his readers.

Meike began to wear a wry smile on her face, sat across from him in her chair. 'Yes… I know who you are,' she said. 'I remember… I'm Meike. Nice to meet you, Alfred from across the street. Heil Hitler!' she added with a twinkle in her eye.

A pause and they both looked at each other with a rising mischief, working out which way to read the moment. *Got it*, their faces decided, breaking out into wide smiles.

'You can sit down if you like, Alfred,' she said, noticing that he had hardly moved since knocking and entering, from a spot half inside and half outside her room.

'Thank you,' he said, taking a polite seat on the edge of her bed.

At closer quarters, the two of them sized each other up, exchanging self-conscious glances followed by nervous smiles and self-deprecating laughs. *So many questions*, Alfred's mind puzzled in odd slow motion. Where does a boy begin with a beautiful girl?

'How have you been?' he said finally, studying her as discreetly as he could.

'Good, Alfred, thank you. Reading… spending time with my grandfather, which has been great, but…' Her answer tailed off. 'I'm going insane trapped in here all day!' she said. 'I can't go out. Someone could report me. I would have to go to hospital… and I would hate that.'

Alfred nodded, uncertain of how to respond. 'Of course,' he said, wanting to say more, but he was falling in love with hearing her speak, the feminine inflection in her voice, its seductive rise and fall. He was spellbound before something pulled at his conscience. 'Could we meet one night... while everyone is sleeping?'

'Oh!' said Meike and Alfred instinctively feared he had ruined his chance. 'I would love that, Alfred,' she added and he couldn't believe it.

II

Alfred was standing outside in the city twilight. It was the night for their secret rendezvous, and he felt a gamut of emotions bubble underneath his surface. He tried to take in the moment he had been waiting for and he looked up at the smudged sky, at beautiful islands of white, like patches on a quilt, moving slowly, a distance apart, across the dusky ocean surrounding them. Alfred wondered at them, breath seeping out his mouth, wispy clouds themselves in miniature, in the night.

He experienced an affinity and he hoped someone else on the planet right now was witnessing the same beauty in the twilight before he watched the patches' white borders lose themselves forever, friends lost in a crowd and blurring with the rest of the night. Twilight was turning to black, and Alfred wriggled his shoulders against the dropping temperature.

Meike's grandparents' house stood now lulled in front of him, but he wasn't ready. He needed still to gather himself and began walking slowly away up the avenue he had grown up on and which he knew so intimately, forming his whole world when he was little. Tonight, it stood different and it unseated Alfred now, dragging his heels along the pavement. He could not consciously recall who that little boy who used to play in the street for hours and hours was. What did he think about the future? Now that it was here, he longed to head back to when his life was simple.

He stood under a streetlight, flashing intermittently, and he looked down at his feet in his best shoes. He found himself pulled back almost magically and he turned back around. *Meike*. He was drawn to her. He looked back up for some comfort, some sign that he was not alone entirely, but the dome of sky overhead was black now, only smudges of deepest blues at its edges.

He was back outside Meike's grandparents' home, turning his head left and then right, and looking along the wide avenue's streetlights and trees, and National Socialist flags, asleep now, too, in the dead of wind. No one. No brown coats or police; no soldiers or drunkards. He was never going to get a better chance.

'Heil Hitler,' he said out loud and he bowed his head briefly. He paced forward, up the two stone steps to the house's front door, which, if everything had gone to plan, would be patiently waiting for Alfred, cracked open. He reached it and he paused. He could not believe what he was about to do. His instincts urged him one last time to turn around, to go home and pull bed covers over himself and fall asleep in bed, precisely where he should be at this hour. Alfred fought the final urge and he carefully reached for the front doorknob and he turned it so slowly, hoping to avoid all sound. The knob began to squeak faintly before the door clicked open. He had done it. *He had done it*. He was in.

Meike stirred in bed, and she realised that she must have fallen asleep. Exhaustion had overcome her. It was a briefly blissful realisation. She had been so spent these last few days that she wished she could stay sleeping deeply for a week and regain her strength fully. She needed every ounce now. In the instant after stirring, she fondly imagined that she was warm and safe in bed at her grandparents'. Her grandmother would lovingly tap on her room door soon, carrying a mug of tea, strong, precisely how she liked it, but her grandmother wasn't coming and Meike struggled to stop herself crying. Her heart ached for her old life.

Meike's new reality flooded over her once more like a sickness. She lay in bed on a large hospital ward. Tomorrow– or today, given the deathly hour – marked day three of her new life. There must have been ten – no, twelve – teenagers housed on the ward where she now was, but she found she had not yet the enthusiasm for her surroundings to make sure. She wanted to close her eyes to everything around her. A clock ticked on the washed-out wall framing the length of the ward behind her. It was tormenting. Too quiet to pick out if you tried, among the cracks of the night, but too loud to ignore if you filled your head with silence only for it to be interrupted by its perfect paces.

Meike grimaced forward in bed and peered to her right. A boy, sick and thin, huddled asleep. His name was Horst, haunted in this life for perhaps thirteen or fourteen years, but if someone had told Meike that he was twenty-three she would not have blinked. Life – or was it death? – seemed to be eating him alive. Yesterday, she began to notice at rare mealtimes that Horst never finished his food. Meike turned herself around as best she could and in the neighbouring bed to her left lay Ingrid, older, stronger, hardened to the hospital surroundings, as if she had been here forever. Ingrid exercised gallows humour, which Meike had not cared for these past two days.

12

Hans and Marta checked that the front door to their home behind them was locked. They looked into each other's eyes. Marta's were frantic, Hans's helpless. They shared silence as they began walking away from their home and heading for the nearest Party offices. Marta caught Hans stealing a glance at her out of the corner of his vision. A thin smile between a husband and wife of all these years. Alone in his head, Hans remembered that during the first Great War, he was a different beast, but now he only felt old, or worse, irrelevant.

Last night, when they had both visited the cinema house, Hans had watched on the newsreels how today's German army obliterated enemies with tanks and planes before infantrymen from warring nations ever came within a thousand yards of each other. Those images in Hans's mind now jarred with the vision before him, entering the endless Party offices in their corner of Berlin. Here, Hitler killed people with paperwork and bureaucrats and desks and eternal offices where nobody, in Hans's short experience, seemed to ever truly be in charge. There was only the will of the Party, whoever was willing that.

'Mrs Richter,' began the Party official, safe behind his desk. 'Please be assured that your granddaughter is in the very best medical hands. We can see happy proof here that she is of the finest German descent. She will be cared for and she *will* return to you once the war is over and our victory over our enemies is complete. Word is that will only be weeks, or a few short months... not years, like before.'

'That's what people in 1914 said,' said Hans and Marta winced, but without daring to look across and scold him with her eyes in public. She could only think of Meike, sat here.

The Party official wanted to roll his eyes.

'We just want to see her... our granddaughter, Meike Steinmann. Let her see a friendly face,' Marta said, subservient to the official. 'It isn't easy for her...' she was about to continue before instinctively feeling Hans's eyes on her. She cut herself short.

'Mrs Richter,' the official said again. 'Please rest easy. Your granddaughter will have the very best care and access to the latest science from the best doctors in the world. Her every need will be cared for.'

Marta closed her eyes and she tried to fight the panic tightening in her chest. This wasn't getting them anywhere. The Party official perched opposite did not offer anything more, instead only adjusting the round spectacles anchoring his face. Marta looked up and she caught the official's eye, holding a smile on her face trapped somewhere between hope and frustration. The official was first to break the silence between them.

He said, after adjusting his spectacles once more, 'Mrs Richter... please go home and focus your efforts and thoughts on your sons currently fighting our enemies. I trust you have sons of fighting age in the army? Our soldiers in the East are currently in great need of winter clothing.'

'We know,' Hans said with a tone.

'We had a daughter,' Marta said. 'No sons.'

The official nodded. 'Your son-in-law,' the official added, looking down at his papers. 'Is he stationed in the East or the West?'

'He...' Marta began.

'Enough, Marta. It's not important,' Hans said.

'He... was arrested... a few weeks ago,' Marta offered. 'We haven't... had word since. It is all a misunderstanding. Abbe was a professor at the university... here in Berlin. He would never... he loves his girls.'

'Enough, Marta,' Hans said with a rising temper.

The official refixed an uncomfortable smile on his face and watched Hans and now Marta rise to their feet and gather themselves.

'We are leaving... good day,' said Hans, placing his hat on his head.

'Yes... yes, thank you for all your help,' Marta said, submissive once more to the official.

'No problem at all. Like I say...' But Hans wasn't waiting to listen and he grabbed Marta's arm sharply.

'Ouch,' Marta said, once they were safely outside.

'How many times, woman?' Hans said. 'You do not need to tell everyone everything!'

13

Meike woke with a start. She immediately realised precisely where she was and, as a result, she could feel her mood crashing. She hitched her frame up as best she could in bed, but her paralysed legs only jolted awkwardly in response, refusing to cooperate. Her bed sheets were clean and crisp, though tangled from a night's sleep. She lifted them and she peered underneath, looking about herself before she did so. She mentally began to nod as she felt beneath her bottom and confirmed that she had not wet herself in the night, or worse. A good start to any day.

'Good morning,' Meike said, seeing Ingrid stirring in bed to her left.

'Morning, Meike,' Ingrid sleepily said and Meike felt her mood improve a little, hitching herself up now more successfully. She let out a sigh. Ten teenagers, she had counted now, on the hospital ward she was on. Each of them had a bedside set of drawers, but they were so cramped that it was impossible to fit anything of consequence inside.

'How did you sleep, Ingrid?' Meike said to her neighbour.

'Like a log,' she said and Meike was only disappointed.

'Don't worry, Meike,' Ingrid said, forcefully shifting her legs together beneath her in bed. 'You will sleep… soon enough. It's strange getting used to so many others being around, isn't it?'

Meike's heart leapt. 'Thanks, Ingrid. Yes… can't seem to sleep a wink in here! I drop off and wake right back up again.'

'I know! I heard you tossing and turning all night.'

Meike frowned in jest. It felt good. 'I thought you slept like a log,' she said.

'Ah, young Meike,' said Ingrid. 'Never give anything away cheaply in here… and don't give any nurse or doctors any satisfaction. They can bugger right off… in their offices at night and frig each other off to their posters of Hitler and Himmler. Oh, Adolf!' Ingrid cried. 'I would help you build the great German race right here, but, oh… you have black hair, Adolf! Why, my Führer? I thought I was supposed to only make love to men with blond hair… and blue eyes?' She acted, placing the flat of her hand against her face theatrically.

'Ha!' Meike laughed.

'Shhhhhhhhh,' hissed others. 'They're coming!'

In bed, Meike calmed herself and tried not to look as a gaggle of nurses strode confidently through the doors to her left and onto the ward, most of them pushing in wheelchairs belonging to patients. Meike remembered they always removed them last thing at night from everyone's bedside and she was still learning to fight the onset of panic each time they did so. Minus her chair to hand, she felt so, so dependent.

Horst, neighbouring Meike to her right, looked openly anxious, furtively lifting his bed covers and glancing underneath, quietly turning his head around to check who was watching, Meike noticed. Finally, Horst pulled his head back out from his covers and wore only horror in his eyes. He then caught Meike's eyes, and she could not help noticing. A ring of damp circled his centre. They both immediately knew. In the night, Horst had wet the bed. *Oh no*, he panicked. *Oh no*.

'It's okay, Horst,' Meike said, but Horst only shook his head at her. He turned around, on display to the rest of the ward and its teenage patients, who all saw the wet patch, like a nightmarish spotlight highlighting his weakness. But nobody laughed.

Meike was about to say something and reach out a hand, but with her chair still to be returned to her by a nurse, she was stuck in bed. She couldn't reach him.

'Horst... Horst!' she hushed, but before she could continue a hand seemed to fall from the heavens and thunder down a slap across his face, felling him instantly. Horst smacked the floor, the sound only somehow underlining the suffocating silence everyone experienced. Meike took in a shocked breath, which Ingrid immediately heard and willed her to hold.

Devil No.2, the hospital's chief nurse who had just slapped Horst, shot a look across to Meike.

'Useless, pathetic boy!' she said, turning back to him as he remained collapsed like a new-born foal on the floor, legs splayed drunkenly. 'Strip your bed this instant and take those sheets to the laundry. And don't even think about putting anything on your feet.'

Horst picked up his frame as meekly as he could, terrified to move any closer to the nurse than he had to. The other patients willed him to stay strong as he stood straight. Devil No.2 glared at him.

'What are you waiting for?' she said, and Horst scurried into panicked action, padding away like a mouse set free by a preying cat. 'Come now,' Devil No.2 then added, dialling down her volume and turning to the rest of the ward. 'Let us not allow our day to be delayed a moment longer.'

The less senior nurses clicked into motion, like wind-up toys. One roughly pushed a wheelchair almost into the side of Meike's bed. Meike looked at the hospital chair she was being forced to adopt and she was filled with small loathing once more. Cumbersome and unsightly, it had not been crafted like the chair her father had lovingly refashioned for her following her accident. She remembered her father smiling deeply at her when he saw her face well with gratitude upon first seeing it.

'Time to get up,' the nurse said to Meike, snapping her out of it, without inviting eye contact.

Under duress, Meike tried to flip her body upright following another bad night's sleep, but it did not react kindly, snapping her back on her bed, her bare ankles and feet shaking. She grimaced in pain.

'Stupid child,' the nurse said. 'Get up… get up, I said.'

Meike was about to shoot the nurse a glare, but instead hid her emotion and bottled it up, safe where no one could steal it like the memory of her father's smile.

14

Anselma felt excited. She was looking forward to attending a Party parade in northern Berlin. Each time in the past weeks she had walked past a poster advertising today's event, she had felt a pinch of a thrill quicken her step. She leant forward to look out of her bedroom window, and overhead she saw the sun splintering through benign, white clouds. Mid-March. Spring was around the corner.

Downstairs, from their kitchen window, Marta gazed out briefly over their modest back garden. Wind rustled tree branches she had grown to know so well over the seasons. All week, she had been quietly dreading attending today's parade, but Hans had shrugged off her doubts, as if *she* was a child.

'Marta, what's the worst it could be?' he had said when Marta had tilted the discussion to the subject after supper the previous evening. 'A brown shirt wearing a cartoon nose? We've seen it all before, haven't we?'

'That doesn't make it right,' Marta had said tartly. 'And that doesn't mean I enjoy seeing it—'

'Are we going?' Anselma suddenly interrupted, entering the kitchen unexpectedly. 'I'm ready.'

'Two minutes,' said Hans, lifting his arms to climb past Anselma in the entrance to their kitchen and forcing Marta to frown. Now she was now being railroaded.

'Five minutes,' she said.

'Two minutes,' Hans mouthed behind his wife's back to a smiling Anselma.

The three of them were walking outside, from their home to a vantage point on the parade route. Marta glanced up. Overhead, the sun shifted behind clouds, like it had been tricking them into venturing out.

'Anselma, I can hear them in the distance,' said Hans and his eldest granddaughter looked at him, eyes flooded with excitement.

She was soon straining on tiptoe, tight in the throng five, six deep, and waiting along the side of the road where the parade promised to pass. Anselma peered up to her right and she could hear the distant cheers carrying on the wind. The sense of anticipation was thrilling. From where she stood, she could see the road bend around to the right. On the wind, the noise grew.

Helped by her height, Anselma first saw the National Socialism flags marching tall in the breeze. Red, black and strong in the Berlin air. She experienced a rush before being jolted briefly out of it by her grandmother, Marta, fidgeting down beside her. Anselma caught a view of Marta's face, uneasy like she was bracing herself for something bad. *Meike*, Marta's mind wondered like a growing seasickness. Today's parade felt like a betrayal.

Anselma turned her attention back around to the road

and suddenly, gloriously, men and women were streaming past in perfect uniform, a brown-shirted army ready to lead the new world.

Behind Anselma, deafening cries of 'Heil Hitler!' crowded Marta's senses. *Why are people so happy?* her head puzzled, *drunk from the onslaught? Has Germany gone mad?* Distaste was churning to worse in her mouth. Surrounded on all sides, she could feel herself struggling to catch a breath.

'Heil Hitler, Mrs Richter!' said Mrs Jaeger, surprising her. Hans turned and instantly saw the distress on his wife's face.

'Heil Hitler, Mrs Jaeger,' he said and instinctively held out an arm to give his wife as much room as was possible within their congested confines.

'Heil Hitler, Mr Richter!' repeated Mrs Jaeger, almost joyous and turning forward away from her. 'So good to see you. Isn't it glorious?'

Marta could not find a reply.

'It is... glorious, Mrs Jaeger,' Anselma said without invitation. 'Glorious,' Anselma repeated, eyes unmoving from the parade as it continued to pass by.

'So handsome too,' Mrs Jaeger nudged her with a wink. 'The men look splendid in their uniforms, don't they?'

Anselma blushed. The young men were taut and purposeful in their brown shirts, which they wore proudly, clean of all conscience, like the world was already theirs. She looked at Mrs Jaeger and they saw themselves in each other.

Behind them, Marta noticed the one person stood in their pocket of the crowd who seemed shorter than her, a little girl, waving a swastika flag in miniature at the front of the throng, blonde curls tumbling onto small shoulders. Marta could not help but see Meike before her, frozen in another life.

The little girl lost control of her flag, stolen from her small grasp on the breeze and whirling away briefly before falling to the ground in front of her. In the path of the parade. Marta knew the girl would dart forward at any moment. The girl sprang out and Marta reacted and shot forward in pursuit, quickly pulling alongside the child, collecting her flag from the roadside. A moment and a smile between them before Marta looked up in horror. A head the size of the moon peered down at her. Marta was too stunned to scream as the head oddly remained perfectly still among the insanity dancing all around them. Marta felt it undressing her with its eyes and she toppled back from her crouching position. She was immediately worried that she might hurt the little girl close beside her but, in the pause, the child was already happily skipping away, back safely to her parents, she noticed out of the corner of her eye. A loud shriek and Marta was able to catch herself. The head moved away.

Marta could now see it was an amateurish construction at garish odds with the unflinching professionalism of the rest of the parade. Beneath the giant heads tottered small, anonymous bodies in cheap business suits, tattered and mocking. Marta reeled again backwards, and Hans moved forward to catch her before the throng did. Suddenly, she was able to take in the real cruelty of the parody and today's Party parade.

The people sporting business rags were on foot, some pedalled stop-start on unicycles, but all wore huge heads toppling precariously above them like they could fall at any moment. Cruel caricatures of Jewish bankers and shopkeepers, monstrous noses crooked and anchoring global features. People cheered. One man with the arm of an American baseball pitcher rifled an orange, brown with mould, at one of the unicyclists. He hit one on the head square on, skittling the individual like a nine-pin to the floor. A wild cheer. And yet Marta only experienced a silent horror. What was this, really? What had Germany become?

The individual who had been floored soon jumped back up, checking their head was still fixed squarely on. Satisfied, the person punched clenched fists triumphant in the air. Another loud cheer from the throng, Anselma was joining in with the euphoria, Marta noticed, before taking a step back and retreating from what she had begun to fear. The pair of them caught each other's eye briefly, uneasily. They could not like what was looking back at them.

Following the parade, the three of them were walking back once more through the front door of their home. Anselma quietly retreated to her room and closed the door to it behind her. She breathed. She opened her eyes and she looked about her room's small furnishings and belongings, which until today had totalled her existence. But now she felt bigger than the thin walls which surrounded her at night and during the day.

She sat politely on her bed, smiled and allowed herself to fall back onto it, arms spread wide like wings. She glanced up, eyes wide, to the room's ceiling and she laughed. Her friends from the League of German Girls occasionally shared illicit swigs from a bottle of schnapps one of them had smuggled into a get-together. Each time the bottle reached her, Anselma never refused a drink, but she always hid how she hated the sensation burning her throat after nauseously swallowing. Now, Anselma felt her whole body tingle with intoxication.

'*Judenrein*,' she said out loud, still lying flat on her back on her bed. '*Judenrein*,' she repeated after hearing the phrase spoken by so many at today's parade.

Unbeknownst to her, Hans was leant on the opposite side of her closed bedroom door, hand poised on the handle, about to tell her that supper was ready. He paused for a breath, and he allowed his hand to continue to feather the handle to Anselma's room. He closed his eyes and let out a sigh. *Judenrein*, his mind replayed, *"clean of Jews"*.

He remembered the feeling when he returned home to Berlin in November 1918, empty and defeated. At the start of the first Great War, Hans proudly marched among four million German men trooping off to war, spirits so high it was like they were already on the road to victory. Four lifetimes later, only half of them returned, found but forever lost. No fanfares greeted them, only feigned smiles from loved ones who now looked like aliens from Mars. Now, led by the National Socialists, Germany was running headlong towards a new catastrophe. Would history forgive her in future?

15

It was morning and Meike was beginning to feel she was settling into life at Hadamar. When she woke earlier, it had been unpleasant, but she was now finding the distaste more palatable than the previous day. Sitting up in bed, she looked across at Ingrid and she experienced a warmth towards her. She couldn't recall meeting anyone quite like her. She found Ingrid exciting.

'Where are we?' she asked Ingrid.

The two of them were up out of bed and sat in their wheelchairs, pushing and mulling around the ward.

'What do you mean, where are we?' Ingrid said, making a face. 'We're in a hospital, for people like *us*.'

'I mean,' said Meike, refraining from rolling her eyes completely. 'Where are we? How far are we from Berlin? I have no idea.'

'Not far,' Ingrid said, nodding. 'Five kilometres from the top of the city. This is Hadamar, it's like a country castle. I was brought here during the day when I first arrived. I saw exactly where we were. Now they take no chances... patients come on buses with the windows blacked out.'

Only five kilometres from Berlin, Meike thought. *Not far, not far from home.*

16

Marta turned her back on her husband Hans in their kitchen. She had expected to feel more, but standing there, busying herself with the breakfast dishes over their sink, it was surprising how little she felt. She had just lied to him. She didn't tell him that she was going this morning to see Dr Jung.

'Heil Hitler, Doctor,' said Marta, entering Dr Jung's office.

'Heil Hitler, Mrs Richter,' the doctor said, head down and continuing to complete his notes from the appointment previous to Marta. 'What can I do for you, Mrs Richter?' he began more warmly, lifting his head to look at her.

Marta paused and took a seat opposite him. Dr Jung waited and tried to maintain a blank face.

'It isn't me, Doctor, it's Meike,' said Marta.

Dr Jung nodded gently. 'What is the problem, Mrs Richter? Was Meike unable to attend herself today?'

'She is seventeen, Doctor,' said Marta, removing her gloves now. 'She was taken away… but I have no idea where. And I really am very frantic, Doctor. I must know she is… safe. I have to know,' she said and then decided to stop herself. She purposefully had not wanted to say too much.

Dr Jung placed the cap on his ballpoint pen and put it down. He took a breath. 'Of course,' he said, regretting not immediately appreciating. 'The new edict… of course, Mrs Richter.'

'Can you help me find Meike?' said Marta.

Dr Jung considered her question and as he did, he thought of Meike. Then, a knock at the door. It was Dr Jung's secretary.

'Doctor, Mrs Jaeger is here for her 11am appointment.'

'Yes… of course she is,' he said, breathing out louder than he had intended. Dr Jung sat for a moment before picking up his pen and making a quick note. 'Thank you, Gertrud.'

His secretary discreetly exited.

'Mrs Richter, I am sorry to hear about Meike, and her no longer being with people she knows. Where is her father, Mr Steinmann, if I may enquire?'

Marta paused and shifted uneasy in her seat. 'He was arrested, Doctor… a few months back, for listening to British broadcasts on his wireless… he would never have been so stupid. We have no idea where he is… how he is,' Marta said.

'Good God,' Dr Jung said, with a furrow knitted in his brow. 'I am very sorry to hear that, Mrs Richter. Abbe is a good man. I have always enjoyed the times I have spent debating issues of the day with him over a late schnapps. It's difficult to know quite where Germany is heading right now, isn't it?' He looked Marta in the eye longer than either of them could recall. Dr Jung was first to look away. 'May I call on you and Mr Richter one evening… this week?' he said.

'Yes… yes, of course, Doctor,' said Marta, overcome but trying to hide her anticipation.

'Thursday, perhaps?' Dr Jung said. 'Is 9pm not too late?'

'9pm is perfect,' Marta said. 'Perfect,' she repeated, but in actual fact more for herself.

Dr Jung looked back at his notes for the morning, and he smiled.

'Would it be an idea to prepare a light supper for us all on Thursday?' she said.

'No… no, please,' said the doctor. 'A nightcap or coffee would be perfect on its own, if that is not too great an imposition.'

Marta smiled. It wasn't.

17

It was daytime and Alfred was walking past the Richters' home. He felt sad, like magic had once captivated the building, but now it was gone. Up above, the sun was failing to break through a dome of grey.

Handsome trees lined the street, branches only occasionally fluttering. When the wind picked up for a moment, a fleeting *whap* from a Nazi flag carried on the air. Alfred had felt impelled to be outside and simply walk, no real direction. His body had simply told him to do it and he had obeyed. Now, looking up, Alfred could start to see beyond the heavy sky and appreciate its myriad shades and shapes.

It was a week after Meike had been taken and today, on his walk, Alfred was reaching new places. He paused for a moment and stood at the edges of Berlin, having intuitively followed a route chosen by the blacked-out buses he and almost everyone in his class at school had witnessed ferrying handicapped youngsters away from their families and their homes, but to where? Alfred stopped walking and completed a full circle, taking in his surroundings – flat fields wide and embracing the rural horizon, and a single, straight road ferrying intermittent traffic into and out of Berlin. For the moment, nothing, no one. Alfred was alone. He walked along the side of the road leading out into the German countryside and he fell into a daydream.

Standing outside, the cold black seemed to be creeping like vines and making Alfred hunch his shoulders tighter. He was unnerved standing outside Meike's grandparents' home in all its slumber. What lay within, at this ungodly hour? Alfred swallowed down an instinct to turn around and dash home, and he grasped hold of the front doorknob to the Richters' property and turned it so slowly he hoped not even to wake sleeping ghosts. Alfred watched his hand work in freeze frame almost, twisting the doorknob agonisingly before the whole frame to the building seemed to magically click open. He had done it. He was in.

He peeked his head beyond the cracked door and into the Richters' home. He could not believe what he was doing. At first glance, everything looked impossibly black before he began to distinguish shades of darkness diluted like a moonlight palette. *Breathe, Alfred*, he counselled himself. He knew he had to turn immediately left and head down a corridor, but everything felt foreboding now in the murk. *Breathe*. Ten strides, face right and he would have reached Meike's bedroom door. And together, they would be together, but Alfred couldn't believe it was about to happen.

He moved one foot and he set off a squeak of a floorboard, and briefly froze. In the tension, everything felt horribly amplified. Stride one. Stride two. Nothing, thank God, and Alfred let out a breath, and then quickly worried that it was too loud. Stride three. Stride four. He paced methodically and finally his eyes were growing attuned, translating the black into charcoal and crimson from carpet he knew from memory lay rich beneath his feet. Stride five. Halfway. *Breathe Alfred.*

Stride five, no, six. Yes, stride six. *Focus Alfred*, he urged himself through clenched fists. Stride seven. A creak beneath his feet again and a moment of panic, but it passed more quickly this time. Stride eight. Stride nine, he paced forward and worried briefly he had overstepped slightly. No, this was it. He was almost there, almost. Ahead on the wall, on his right side, Alfred made out the skeleton of a door, Meike's bedroom door. Ten. *Stride ten*, Alfred repeated in his head for confirmation. Then chaos.

18

'Good evening, Doctor,' said Marta, opening her front door to Dr Jung and trying to contain her excitement.

'Good evening, Mrs Richter,' the doctor said, removing his hat and waiting a polite moment before entering the home. Marta closed the front door behind their guest and then led him through to Hans, sat waiting in their study. Hans climbed out of his chair and held his hand out warmly to Dr Jung.

'Hans,' said Dr Jung.

'Doctor,' said Hans.

'Erich, please.'

'A drink, Doctor?' said Marta. 'There is coffee made fresh in the kitchen, or something with Hans?'

Dr Jung, who had an early start tomorrow, was conflicted. 'A small… schnapps, please,' he said.

Hans walked over to their drinks cabinet and identified a decanter containing their best schnapps. He topped up his own glass and then poured a generous finger for their guest.

'A little water with it, Erich?'

'A little… thank you,' he said politely.

Marta returned to the room with a coffee for herself, anxious for the business of the hour to begin. The three of them were soon seated, each happily with a drink at hand. Marta looked at Dr Jung.

'Mrs Richter, Hans,' he said. 'Meike, as you know and, of course, had to unfortunately experience, was taken away because of her age. She is seventeen and she is included in the new law for all youngsters to be housed and cared for by the state in hospital while we remain at war.' Dr Jung, keeping half an eye on Marta's expectant face, knew he must pick his words with care. 'Mrs Richter, Hans—' he continued, allowing himself a pause.

'Another small schnapps, Doctor?' Marta then interrupted nervously.

'That would be very kind,' he said. He continued, 'The Nazis, I believe, are targeting minorities in Germany. I would like to strongly add that I do not know Mrs Richter, Hans. I do not have unequivocal proof and yet many of us in the medical profession have been in a privileged position to foresee early warning signs. I can, if you will allow, form a bigger picture in my head.'

Dr Jung sipped from his glass as Marta nodded in reply. Hans remained silent.

'Coloured men and women are being identified and they are not being encouraged to enter wedlock and bear children. Homosexuals too… like a condition which can be cured. The handicapped, either physically or of the mind, will not be allowed to marry and have children. They are being sterilised, so they are unable in future to even have a choice.'

A telltale pattering outside on windows. It had begun to rain. Distracted briefly, Dr Jung turned back to the room and to his hosts this evening.

He said, 'I fear National Socialism would like to wheedle such elements out of German society. And there will be others, no doubt. Jews, of course, gypsies. The Nazis want women who can have children... lots of healthy children. And men who are physically capable... who can work and who can fight.'

Dr Jung finished his drink and raised his eyes at Hans and finally at Marta, and he could not hide sadness in his half smile.

'Do you know anything about Meike, Doctor?' said Marta. 'Have you found out anything... anything at all?'

Hans winced at his wife's directness and was about to roll his eyes.

'Not specifically, I am afraid,' Dr Jung said, and Marta felt her spirits sinking. 'But. But, Mrs Richter, Hans, I have made enquiries with doctors I am still close to... who I can be discreet with. Sadly, most of the senior physicians in Berlin are now loyal to the Party. It would be dangerous for me... and dangerous potentially for Meike.'

Marta shifted back upright in her chair and Hans, sensing the moment, reached out a hand and placed it softly on top of hers. A smile passed between them, and Dr Jung felt he was intruding on the moment.

He lowered his head and he continued to speak. 'I know who many of them are, but very many are not real doctors, in a pure sense. They have little formal training... they will simply do what they are told, what the Party tells them, to give Party policies the 'backing' of science. It is perhaps why,

Mrs Richter, Hans, I remain a relatively unimportant general practitioner, in a relatively unimportant post in Berlin.'

A breath and Dr Jung lifted his drink to his mouth and emptied it down his throat. He nodded to his hosts after placing it back down on the table between them. Anselma, head down, suddenly entered the room casually in a dressing gown. She was immediately surprised to see a guest and Dr Jung, no less, with her grandparents at this hour, and she quickly wrapped her gown around herself more tightly. Marta frowned, which Dr Jung could not help but notice, and climbed from her chair, leaving Hans and their guest seated.

'Anselma,' she began. 'Let's leave your grandfather and Dr Jung alone. There is some paperwork for them to deal with regarding your sister. Are you hungry? Can I fix you some supper?'

'I'm fine, Grandmother,' she said, uneasy. 'I am going to bed.'

Marta nodded. 'Sleep well, my dear.'

'Good night, Anselma,' Dr Jung called across politely, feeling it was correct to do so.

'Good night, Doctor. Heil Hitler,' she said.

'Yes,' said the doctor. 'Heil Hitler.'

Marta returned to the two of them. 'Apologies, Doctor,' she said. 'May I fill your glass?' she said.

'Yes,' he said, raising and handing her his glass. 'Half full, Mrs Richter. That is very kind.'

'Doctor, please continue,' Marta said, placing a glass down fuller than half full for their guest. Hans was not offered another drink, they both noticed, happy to share a lighter moment with their eyes. Back to business.

'Yes, I was explaining,' Dr Jung said. 'There are seven hospitals or centres nationally in Germany currently designated by the Party to take youngsters, up to the age of seventeen, with mental or physical handicaps, like Meike. The closest to us here in Berlin is Hadamar, about ten kilometres north.'

Marta looked, eyes wide and hopeful at Hans, who worked hard to mirror Marta's response in his face.

'But I am afraid, Mrs Richter, Hans,' he said, 'that I have no idea which hospital Meike is in. I don't know and the Party has too deeply divided the profession for me to find out.'

Dr Jung paused and drank from his glass, the alcohol warming him happily. Marta secretly smiled at him. In the intimacy of his visit, her instincts had decided they liked him even more.

'Children like Meike are selected,' he said and Marta, hands wrapped around her cooling coffee cup, disliked the word "selected".

'Selected... how, Doctor?' she said.

'Good question. For a patient like Meike, in her circumstance,' Dr Jung spoke, treading carefully with his words, which was not lost on Marta. 'Three doctors, friendly to the Party, each receive a form. All the Party needs is two of them to consent to the patient being taken into care while we are at war.'

Marta scoffed quickly in disgust. Dr Jung pursed his lips in sympathy at Marta before quickly pressing on.

'The information will be passed to the relevant authorities, who act on it and go and collect the patient.'

'Take,' Marta said. 'Meike was taken from us, Doctor.'

Dr Jung nodded diplomatically and the three of them shared silence for a moment before a small clock on the room's mantelpiece surprised them rather by chiming that it was 11pm. Dr Jung was grateful for the cue.

'Mrs Richter, Hans, I really should be getting home. It's late. It's time I left you in peace for the evening.'

'Of course, Doctor... of course,' said Marta, rising from her seat and picking up and holding his glass, along with her coffee cup, ready to take through to their kitchen.

'Thank you... thank you,' she said, and Dr Jung nodded at her a final time, raising his hat as Hans saw him out.

19

It was late and it was dark. Dusk was no longer distinguishable in the fragments of sky visible from the hospital ward's high windows. Meike woke and she immediately remembered where she was. *This* place. She hated that moment of realisation flooding her with unhappiness for the seconds and minutes which painfully followed. She was quickly becoming exhausted, having to overcome the depression in miniature each time. Like everything at Hadamar, happiness was a struggle.

From the ward's tall windows, Meike's eyes traced moonlight slanting along each bed like searchlights inverted, seeking strays only in Berlin's underbelly, but Meike could hear no British bombers raiding overhead. Her bed was one of five along the longest flank of the ward, opposite a mirroring five running along the ward's parallel wall. Meike shuffled beneath her bed sheets. She feared she could not recall her family's faces. What was happening to her?

Meike's hand reached out from under her bed sheets and she clasped a metal rail which was cold. The bar ran higher than her mattress along the side of her bed and it enabled her to pull herself up. Out of the corner of her eye in the neighbouring bed she recognised a shift. Horst. *Horst!* Was he actually, finally back?

'Horst... Horst!' Meike whispered through the dark. 'Horst, you're back, welcome back!'

'Hi, Meike.' And there it was. He *was* back, but his voice carried a hollowness. 'Nice... to hear you, Meike,' he said.

Meike tried to pull herself quietly up in bed, but it was difficult to guard against her bed clanging rudely as she fidgeted. If the nurses on shift heard her...

'Where have you been?' Meike hissed excitedly.

'In... another... part of the hospital,' he said, his tone heavy like a drunk.

'Horst, are you okay?' she said. 'We've been worried... we didn't know where you were... what had happened.'

Meike managed to heave herself upright in bed, so that she could turn more easily towards Horst, her eyes now accustomed to the black. She took his face back in but was only startled. She was glad of the dark to cloak her alarm.

'Meike... I don't feel well. I should sleep. It will be morning soon. The nurses will be here. I will have to get up,' he said.

'I know, Horst. I'm sorry,' she said and caught his eyes in hers for a moment. They were Horst's eyes, but they protruded from the rest of his face, more skeletal than before and like his whole body was beginning to belong to someone else entirely. Meike could see his limbs had locked, which only underlined his current anxiety.

In the sober light of morning, Horst did not look better to Meike, watching him with a wince as a nurse barked at him impatiently.

20

'Must we really have the Beckers over for dinner this evening?' Hans said to Marta in their kitchen.

'Yes, we must,' she said with a tone suggesting that, for once, she might not disagree with her husband. She was already dressed for dinner and ready to greet their guests, busying herself in their kitchen, checking cold starters and roasting in the oven an offcut of lamb, a great luxury these days. The glorious smell filled the kitchen as she opened the oven door, but then nobody complimented her on her cooking quite like Meike and the sadness of that silence interrupted her briefly. *Not tonight*, she told herself.

'Hans, go upstairs and change. The Beckers will be here soon.'

'Yes... yes,' he said. 'Please try and relax, Marta,' he added, turning around to face her. 'It's dinner, just dinner. I want you to enjoy this evening.'

'I know... I know,' Marta said. 'Go!' she added playfully, trying to lighten the mood.

'Going,' he agreed, raising his hands in happy surrender. 'Heil Hitler!' he said with a wink.

'Heil Hitler!' one of their guests, Harri Becker, soon snapped, clicking his heels like only a professional soldier could.

'Heil Hitler,' said Marta awkwardly as everyone gathered in the Richters' living room.

'Heil Hitler,' greeted Mr and Mrs Becker.

'Heil Hitler!' said Anselma, walking in and the last to join the party, her eyes attracted to Harri in his army uniform.

Hans had a schnapps safely inside him, from a small flask tucked upstairs in his sock drawer. He wondered glibly if the army used cardboard these days to fashion uniforms, Harri's appeared so stark before him. Far from the woollen tunics he and the men in his battalion wore during the first Great War. Hans remembered removing layers of his uniform prior to a big push, so that he could be light on his feet.

He felt his wife's hand on his arm, transporting him back to the present with a start. He sensed her feeling bone beneath thinning muscle, as if growing old was a secret he was not ready to share. Even with his wife.

'Hans!' Marta said cheerily. 'Fix Mr Becker a schnapps.'

'Of course, of course,' Hans repeated, moving over to their drinks cabinet. 'How many fingers, Ludwig?'

'One, please,' he said. 'With a dash of water.'

'Erika. Would you like wine now? Or something else before we eat?' Marta said.

'Whatever you are drinking, Marta, will be perfect.'

'Harri, what is it like helping defeat our enemies in the East?' Anselma asked and nobody said anything for a moment.

'It is not as I had imagined,' he said.

Harri's parents smiled thinly, like part of their son was still somewhere off in the East and not here in the room with them. Hans mirrored the silence and held his drink like a shield, and the four oldest people in the room sunk their gaze to the floor briefly and the brave carpet Marta had never quite cared for.

'Please tell me how terrible our enemies are,' Anselma pushed Harri a second time.

Marta frowned but felt bound by the others' tacit acceptance of her question.

'They are...' Harri began. 'They are...'

'How long have you been at the front, Harri?' Hans asked and Harri was glad of the direct question.

'Six months,' he said, taking the opportunity to light a cigarette through an already seasoned squint. 'This is my first leave home. I have two weeks.'

Hans nodded. Six months was plenty long enough, he knew that.

'You and the Sixth Army are just getting started,' Harri's father Ludwig jumped in, like an unwelcome slap on the back. Ludwig smoked a cigarette from a silver case he had not offered around the room, Hans noted. 'Those Slavs had better hop smart east, to Moscow,' Ludwig said. 'That whole hinterland is rightfully ours. We need it to expand our industry, our workforce.'

'You didn't fight in 1914, did you, Ludwig?' Hans said and Marta closed her eyes as discreetly as she could to display her disapproval to her husband. *'Please don't talk about the war... the Great War,'* she had said earlier this morning while they finished breakfast. *'Of course,'* Hans had said without looking up.

'Shall we go through?' said Marta, desperate to turn the conversation elsewhere. 'Dinner is ready.'

'Lovely, Marta,' said Erika, quickly glancing at her husband.

'It all feels very old hat, don't you agree, Hans – the Great War?' Ludwig said, walking through to the Richters' dining room. 'All those lines and trenches and stalemates. Thank goodness for industry and technology. We can make it pay against these Slavs and Jews… the bloody French.'

'Darling, please,' said Erika, putting out her cigarette politely as Marta began serving starter plates. 'Marta has prepared dinner for us this evening. Let us enjoy it.'

Harri and Anselma were the last of the six-strong party to walk through to the dining room decorated especially for the occasion by candlelight. 'Beautiful,' Hans secretly mouthed to Marta as they sat. 'Thank you,' she mouthed back before blowing her eyes up at him and tilting her head in reference to talk of the war.

I know, I know, Hans's face replied with a gentle nod.

'Where is Meike this evening?' Erika questioned and Marta held her composure, but Hans could see her hackles rise.

'She is in an institution, where she can be with others in her situation while we remain at war,' she answered carefully. 'We visit her at weekends. It's a marvellous place, really… marvellous. She really is quite content there, I think,' Marta said before taking a mouthful of red wine and checking in with Hans with her eyes. He looked surprised.

'In her situation… of course,' said Erika. 'It sounds for the best. It must be such a strain for you all.'

'No strain,' Marta said. 'We marvel at how wonderfully Meike has dealt with everything after the accident… don't we, Hans?' she said, crying out for support.

'She is a real soldier, that one,' Hans said without thinking, but Erika took offence.

'It is so good to have a fighting son today,' she said. 'Whom one can correspond with for latest news from the front. Not second hand, like the headlines one watches at the cinema house.'

'War is *never* like the newsreels at the cinema houses,' Hans said, and Erika refrained from eating for a moment, placing her knife and fork to the side of her plate. She picked up her napkin to dab her mouth, as the candlelight, standing in the middle of the table, flickered with a draft creeping in from outside.

'Why don't we let Harri speak?' Anselma said, and nobody at the table objected. 'Harri, tell us what it's *really* like fighting this second Great War?'

Harri had anticipated the question all day. Now it was here, he needed nicotine to help him answer it, lighting a cigarette from a holder he kept in his breast pocket. He took a drag of his cigarette and was quickly reminded of relaxing and smoking with soldiers in his unit, during a pause in the push towards Stalingrad. It may as well have been the moon, it felt so far. In silence, Harri continued to smoke, his parents waiting uneasily. Their son was still so young.

He finally stubbed out the small of his cigarette, but he could feel the welling rising. Tears, rolling softly down from his eyes, perfectly calm amid impossible emotion, like the Slavs Harri's CO ordered men from his unit to shoot and kill. *Kill them, corporal.*

'*Kill them corporal!*' Harri's imagination vividly now recalled, making him jump and only wing a Jewish gentleman, days short of his ninetieth birthday. Five paces before him. So close it was like he was family. The old man groaned as if he was only winded, not shot and all the while, back at the Richters' dining room, tears trickled down Harri's cheeks. Still, he made no sound.

'You must get Meike, Mrs Richter. You must,' he hushed, eyes bowed.

Deep frowns drew across the foreheads of Harri's parents as they exchanged heavy eyes.

'Enough of this nonsense,' his mother said, but Marta couldn't quite believe what he had said.

'Harri, what did you say?' said Marta.

'Mrs Richter, you must get your granddaughter,' Harri said again.

'That is enough, Harri!' his mother scolded. 'I think it really is time we left, Ludwig,' she said, picking herself up abruptly to her feet and shooting a look at her husband, who duly obeyed. 'Harri is clearly not himself at the moment. We must apologise,' Mrs Becker added unapologetically. 'Exhaustion, simple exhaustion, you understand. Harri just needs rest.'

'Yes... of course, Mrs Becker,' Hans said, sparking sharp eyes from Marta.

'No, Hans,' Marta said with a firmness he could not recall. 'Harri, please speak clearly,' Marta said. 'What are you trying to say?'

'Tssskkkk,' Erika said, busily placing her cigarettes and lighter back in her handbag. 'Enough of this. Harri can't help Meike, Marta. She is where she is...'

'How dare you?' Marta said. 'Get out... get out now.'

Erika stood next to her son and pulled him by his collar like he was a stray cat.

'You must get Meike, Mrs Richter... you must,' Harri said once more, stumbling away in his mother's hold.

'That is enough, Harri!' his mother said, her face now red with rage.

'This is not like 1914, Mr... Mrs Richter,' Harri said. 'It's not...'

Crack. And a gasp from Anselma, who rushed her hand to her mouth too late to catch whatever had fallen from it. In front of everyone, in varying distress, Erika had slapped her son.

With Harri still in rough tow, she paced out the Richters' front door, quickly pursued by Ludwig, who raised his eyes to Hans in apology. Marta and Hans stood in their doorway and watched, while Anselma remained behind them and looked on.

'What did he mean?' Marta looked at Hans, standing on their doorstep and half watching the Beckers unceremoniously climb into their car. 'What did Harri mean, saying this is not a war like before?'

Hans remained silent.

'What did he mean, Hans?' she repeated, turning squarely on to him, and also allowing her eyes to take in Anselma, who also stood mute. 'Oh, you're no use, both of you!' Marta wrapped her arms around herself against the night and turned back inside, leaving them both where they stood. 'Think of your sister, Anselma, think of where she is right now...' Marta said, her voice trailing off along with her footsteps down their home's front corridor.

Hans looked at Anselma and he shook his head softly. *Not now.*

Anselma shrugged at Hans, who wasn't sure what to make of the reaction, but there had been enough emotion for one evening. Hans turned around and he watched Anselma walk and turn upstairs to her bedroom. He felt exhausted all of a sudden.

He walked carefully back inside up their hallway, baulking from continuing on to their kitchen, where he could hear Marta angrily tackling this evening's dinner plates. He paused to his left, steadying himself with an arm on the doorframe and he peered, waist up, back into their dining room, and the scene of tonight's drama. *All quiet now*, he reported in his head to himself.

Stood above him, Anselma had paused too, reaching a supporting hand out onto the banister and grounding herself momentarily on their stairs. She looked down at her grandfather, who surprised her by glancing up and making eye contact. The two of them held each other's gazes uncertainly. Then they both heard. Sobs, soft at first before becoming more pronounced. In their kitchen, Marta was crying.

Anselma continued to look at her grandfather, standing outside their dining room, frozen by his wife's distress. The pain began to write itself across his face and in that moment, he felt it. The size of their home had doubled with only the three of them within it, without Meike.

The following morning, Marta awoke and experienced only empty regret. Her world felt out of balance, like she was on a ship trapped forever in a storm. Routine tasks like finishing last night's supper dishes, following the previous evening's disastrous dinner, were more of an effort. Marta began boiling water in a kettle on their stove for coffee, but this morning none of its usual noises, like the gush of water from the tap or the liquid bubbling happily to a boil, lifted her mood. She was flat, like the fields in Holland which had been discussed every night this week on the wireless, now overrun with invading German soldiers and a world away from the summers she and Hans had spent there when they were magically still so uncertain of each other.

Marta took a seat, her reward, supper plates and pots all clean again, at their kitchen table and sipped a mug of breakfast coffee. She felt old and tired. A flicker in her mind's eye and morning's first light catching on her husband's face during those weeks in Holland, like the whole universe gravitated around them. This place was the centre of everything.

Marta stood up and walked sadly back to their kitchen sink, underwhelmed and small. Her eyes were sore from lack of sleep. She watched now that same man, her husband, shuffle outside in their back garden in his dressing gown, smoking the one cigarette of the day, first thing, she still allowed him. He was soon hacking forward from the tar which aggravated the scars fingering his lungs from a gas attack on the German line he defended so bravely in 1918. Four years earlier, he had left her invincible that July, she remembered so clearly, before the world had swallowed him whole and spat back a man she found it hard to recognise.

She watched Hans slowly catch his breath and steady himself, hands on his knees for extra support. He smoked the last of his cigarette, which he wasn't about to discard lightly, and stubbed out the final butt on the sole of his house slippers. He turned and his look easily connected with hers, like it always did. Like he knew. She needed him now more than ever.

21

Mid-morning at the hospital, immediately prior to the doctor's daily rounds. Meike and the other patients on the ward all wore anxious faces. Who would be the unwanted focus of the doctor's attention today? Meike felt her stomach churn. She could not escape the selfish emotion that she did not wish to draw the doctor's focus herself and yet, why should it not be her and be someone else? Out of the corner of her eyes, she looked heavenward briefly.

Meike finished her breakfast. It was time to haul herself out of bed and push to the bathroom. She could already feel the daily dread of her toilet routine rising in her chest. Meike looked down at her pretty belly button, peeping out from below her tousled nightshirt, the landmark on her skin marking where her feeling stopped following her accident. At least that was a rare bright spot of being in hospital and Hadamar. She could talk about visiting the toilet here with other patients like Ingrid and Horst, who naturally understand her and its delicacy.

Meike inched herself up in bed and she threw crisp linen off her bare legs and feet in a deliberate toss. Her cold bones flipped her suddenly back in a juddering spasm. Thankfully, no day nurses were yet on the ward. It was December and outside Meike could hear birdsong, oblivious to surrounding human circumstance; Meike appreciated it calmly for a moment. She closed her eyes.

She heaved herself back upright, struggling initially against the tide of her spasm, pushing off doubled-up pillows behind her propping her up. She surveyed her ankles, tilting her head like they represented a corner to look around. They had largely returned to a flattering teenage size overnight, but she knew that would not last. Gravity was rarely her friend, her eyes rolled.

She grabbed once more the edges of the bed sheets and threw them clear of herself successfully this time. She started to smile in small triumph. From the neighbouring bed, Ingrid watched Meike haul herself up and begin transferring into her chair, which a hospital nurse had placed by her bedside a short while earlier, at the start of the daytime shift.

Ingrid turned her eyes away from Meike, allowing her the dignity of transferring into her chair without an audience, glancing down casually instead toward the hospital ward's white floor and at her stockinged feet. She wiggled her elegant, long toes in her imagination, and she smiled, half in pleasure and half in jest, that she could no longer physically perform the action. She turned back to Meike and saw her struggling to inch herself closer to her bedside, her white nightie falling short at pink, puffy thighs. Ingrid admired her in the moment, remembering herself briefly in those days of long, waking nightmares in the wake of her accident, after she had lost her legs, as she bluntly always put it to people. Her mother always corrected her.

'*You haven't lost them, darling, they are right here,*' she heard her mother repeat now. *Who was she really protecting?* Ingrid thought.

Nurses suddenly busily appeared in a buzz at the top of the ward, interrupting Ingrid's imagination. They were preparing for the doctor's morning rounds. At Hadamar, it was a trial for everyone. A nurse quickly stood at Meike's bedside, prompting her to transfer into her chair. But her secret T-shirt to soak up any spills in the night still lay crumpled beneath her, before Meike tugged it clear as the nurse looked away.

Meike's face creased in panic when she spotted it was soiled with a circle of damp. She looked to her left and to Ingrid, busy practising wheelies in her chair and then to her right, but there was only the nurse, whose eyes immediately met Meike's. The nurse softly shrugged her shoulders and smiled, making Meike breathe in relief rather too loudly and the nurse motioned with her eyes for Meike to hide her T-shirt in her bedside cupboard. Meike listened and hurried the garment away.

'Come to think of it, let me wash that for you first,' the nurse whispered.

Thank you, Meike wanted to mouth with all her soul, naming her new ally Angel No.1. We had Devil No.1 and Devil No.2. *Why not?* Meike thought.

'The doctor is here,' the nurse said out loud to Meike, but refusing to break her focus away from fixing Meike's sheets as best she could in the time available.

'Nurse,' the doctor soon spoke, walking past Angel

No.1, finishing up. Devil No.1 was as wide as he was short, with jowls beneath his chin like a walrus. The hospital's nurses, led by Devil No.2, trailed him like worshippers, as he approached Ingrid.

'How are you today, Ingrid?' he said with half a wall up.

'I am fine, Doctor, thank you… Heil Hitler,' she said, holding her eyes straight. Some of the nurses exchanged glances.

'I am glad to hear it, Ingrid. Heil Hitler,' the doctor said, not looking up from his notes.

'Who is next?' he asked out loud with a confidence Meike did not care for.

'Meike Richter, Doctor,' Angel No.1 said simply.

'Thank you, Nurse,' Devil No.2 said like the question had not been meant for her. 'Ah, yes,' said the doctor, who appeared on good form. 'I do hope you are settled, Meike Richter,' he continued, but Meike did not know how to reply before the doctor turned his attention to Meike's other neighbour, Horst.

Horst stood cowed and fearful before Devil No.1, who stepped forward a pace, making Horst flinch. Horst had only pyjama bottoms on his bones. No shirt. Only scrawn.

'Nurse, come forward,' the doctor said, not taking his eyes off Horst, standing before him, and not turning around to look at Hadamar hospital's chief nurse, Devil No.2, who now stepped forward to join them. 'Help me make a point while we have our audience,' the doctor said.

Ingrid turned her eyes to the floor.

'You will watch, child!' Devil No.2 said, turning around to address Ingrid. 'This is why… this is why you are all here… to sort the weak from the strong, who can contribute to our Führer's Reich.'

Meike experienced an unseating panic as she watched. And waited.

'I will grab one leg,' the doctor said before he began communicating to Devil No.2 only with nods and small whispers. Suddenly, he and Devil No.2 each had Horst by one ankle, hanging him aloft and upside down like a wild rabbit, trapped in a snare. Horst was flipped hopelessly backwards, his head catching the floor with a thud, which made the other patients want to retch.

Meike gasped and immediately clasped her hand over her mouth. Angel No.1 ballooned her eyes at her, an exchange which didn't go unnoticed by Devil No.2. Meike moved her hand away slowly from her mouth, like she could help Horst in some way. She kept her eyes fixed forward on the horror, and she tried to hold her breath, but Ingrid could only look away. She had seen enough.

Horst continued to dangle upside down, rocking gently now in the air as Devil No.1 and Devil No.2 each held him with a grip at arm's length, like they might catch something were he to sway too close to them.

'Nurses, look at this boy,' the doctor said, keeping his focus on Horst. 'He is sixteen, according to our records, and yet anyone would think he was only a child of twelve or thirteen. Do you think *he* can contribute to our Führer's Reich?'

A pause and one or two glances among the group of spectating nurses huddled together in the centre of the ward.

'No,' the nurses answered in rehearsed unison.

'I didn't hear you,' the doctor said, pushing his spectacles up the bridge of his nose, but all the time, keeping his eyes on Horst.

'No,' the nurses repeated more loudly.

'Good,' said the doctor, then helping to toss Horst back on his bed like a piece of meat.

'Let us continue, let us continue,' he said, pacing away quickly.

22

It was morning and Marta was in a hurry to leave the house early. She did not want to see Hans or Anselma, both still to climb from their beds and show their faces for the day, before she left. She pulled a scarf around her neck as she paced to the front door, closing it behind her with relief. She had succeeded. She could be alone for a few hours. Her mind, still creased from last night's ill feeling, was grateful.

She walked away, down the short steps leading up to their home and out into the suburban avenue, picking up her feet in the direction of their local church. She wanted to speak to her priest.

She creaked open the wooden door to the church, peering around it uncertainly. It wasn't a Sunday. The thick wooden door was reassuring to touch. It smelt old, and Marta's subconscious cherished the sense that each time she entered church there was something greater than her and her life on this Earth. There was a reassurance in that.

The building's cool air only reminded her that the space was special, the light happily dim, quiet. Marta closed the door softly behind her as always seemed one's duty. Figures busied themselves out of sight discreetly. None looked up, except Father Maier, whose sermons she listened to fondly each Sunday. His face was beautifully ugly, crooked features forged only from kindness. He looked at you like you were God's creation.

'Mrs Richter,' he said, walking towards her with a wide smile.

'Father,' she said, unwrapping the scarf from her neck. 'I was hoping to take a little of your time this morning. Can I speak with you?'

A moment of silence between the two of them. This was not usual.

'Of course, of course,' he said casually. 'Please sit, Mrs Richter... I seem to be busy doing nothing this morning.'

Marta smiled politely at the self-effacement. The two of them each took a seat and Marta felt the age of the pew beneath her. A "Heil Hitler", sharper than it should have sounded in the distance, caught their attention and caused them to turn their heads towards it before Father Maier shouldered responsibility for the interruption, turning to Marta and raising his palms in apology. Marta smiled genuinely. There was relief for her that she was here, alone. *Meike*, her imagination called out softly.

'What would you like to talk about, Mrs Richter?'

'Meike, Father,' she began. 'I fear... she is in danger. But I don't know where she is, or what to do. She was taken from us, and it has always felt wrong to me that we – I – should not be allowed to go and see her. It's not easy for her, it's never easy for her... and she doesn't have her father currently. It's only us, myself and Mr Richter.'

Father Maier nodded gently and yet he did not answer her out loud, unseating Marta ever so slightly.

She continued, 'I have heard rumours, Father, that patients like Meike are not safe… they're not safe where they are. The Party maybe cannot be completely trusted… like everyone thinks.'

More nods from Father Maier but, again, nothing more.

'Last night, Father, we had guests for dinner,' Marta explained. 'The Beckers, if you know them. Towards the end of the evening, Harri, their son, who is fighting in the army in the East, grew agitated… he was quite upset, Father. He told us that this war is not like the others… it's not like the Great War Mr Richter fought in. Have you heard anything, Father?' she asked, eyes hopeful.

Father Maier looked at her and he saw quiet desperation. A creak of a movement, elsewhere in church, made Father Maier's eyes turn away again, pulling them out of the intimacy of their exchange and Marta feared the moment she had been carefully building to, in the last few minutes, was lost before Father Maier nodded, more definitely now.

'I do not say this lightly, Mrs Richter, and please accept that I share this with you in the strictest confidence.'

'Of course,' said Marta.

'I have heard, yes, that, as you say, our soldiers are not fighting a… traditional war in the East. This is a war of faith, Mrs Richter.'

Marta tried to take in what she was being told, but she felt she was missing something. Father Maier saw that she remained unsure, and he nodded, casting his eyes down momentarily.

'You would do very well, Mrs Richter, if I can say, to speak with Mrs Kohler... at the earliest opportunity, the earliest.' He reached out a soft hand and placed it gently, like a benign shield, on top of Marta's hand. She looked down. She wasn't sure what to feel. In all these years, she had never been this close to him before.

'Thank you, Father,' she said, nodding and closing her eyes for a moment. By the time she opened them again, it was like the conversation between them just now had never happened. Like a flock of birds disturbed, the secrecy was gone, and their prior politeness restored.

23

Meike was sat up in bed, trying to eat her breakfast, but she wasn't doing a very good job. She glanced across again to the neighbouring bed on her right, Horst's, like he might magically appear, but nothing, no one, only an eerily vacated place where someone she once knew had slept. His bed was perfectly made. Meike looked back at Ingrid and the worry in their faces mirrored each other's. Where was he? What had happened to him, their friend?

Everything felt so clean on the ward today. Meike thought she could taste antiseptic on her tongue, which wasn't helping her appetite. Already, she could not stomach her breakfast, sat unappealingly beneath her on a white hospital tray. She knew she would be hungry later, but right now she didn't care, she wanted her friend, Horst.

'Eat something, Meike, please,' the kind nurse said, now busy at her bedside. No Devil No.2 this morning. But Meike only continued to push her food around her plate.

'Never mind,' the kind nurse said, deciding to take her breakfast plate away. 'Let's go get you weighed for the week… so your records are up to date.'

'Okay,' Meike said simply.

'Let's go,' the kind nurse said, after helping Meike transfer to her chair, which did not go unnoticed by Ingrid. The kind nurse then took the liberty of beginning to push Meike in her chair off the ward without first asking. Meike, for once, did not mind. The pace of being pushed perked her up.

'Later, Ingrid,' she said as she travelled past her neighbour's bed, the kind nurse weaving her and her chair in between dirty bedding thrown liberally on the ward floor, ahead of being taken to the laundry. Ingrid watched the pair of them press through the ward's double doors, announcing a quieter corridor containing offices and supporting rooms.

Angel No.1 and Meike entered the office belonging to Devil No.2, where patients were weighed each week. It was uninspiring. The kind nurse pushed Meike up onto metal scales in the room, large enough to sit both a patient and their chair, the weight of which was deducted from the final reading.

'You've lost 3lb this week, Meike,' the kind nurse frowned. 'You must eat, Meike… you must.'

But there was no reply from her patient.

'Are you getting enough to eat? Is that the problem, Meike?' the nurse said, with Meike still perched up on the scales.

'Yes,' she said instinctively, but not entirely truthfully. 'Some supper in the evening would be nice… a change, but the food's fine.'

'Okay… okay,' Angel No.1 said unconvinced but realising the conversation wasn't going anywhere and, anyway, keen that they were both safely back on to the ward in time for the doctor's daily rounds. The kind nurse helped her patient off the scales before Meike's eyes were pulled back, like clothing snagged on a hook, spying something on Devil No.2's desk. Words, indented and jumping out from a paper, read, *400 idiots x 5,000 reichsmarks = 2 million reichsmarks per year.*

Meike's mind puzzled.

'What's that?' she said to the kind nurse, who turned and noticed herself the papers which had caught Meike's attention. Angel No.1 could see the National Socialist eagle emblazoned at the top of them, warning enough for her to pry no closer.

24

Sunday. Marta walked out of church, not feeling entirely refreshed as she normally did this time each week. The doubt nagged at her as she navigated more quickly than usual the pockets of people stood speaking casually and relaxing in the very feeling presently eluding her. Marta was upset, if she was being truthful. She cherished hearing Father Maier speak for these precious moments each Sunday and yet, today, her head had been elsewhere. Mrs Kohler.

Marta had spotted her, finally, after anxiously being one of the first to take their seat in church this morning. Marta's head had been spinning, like the times she drank too much schnapps as a teenager. The sensation had thankfully stopped when she had spotted Mrs Kohler, taking a pew politely towards the end of one aisle, removing her gloves as she sat. She had a neat and tidy appearance, Marta noticed, before pulling her gaze away for fear of causing offence.

An impatient hour later, Marta began to anxiously shuffle out of church, trapped in a corridor of feet and shoes beneath her, some scuffed, others shining. She lifted her eyes to see better where she was going. Up ahead, a nod and a smile here and there, Father Maier dutifully waiting, bidding thanks and farewell for seven more days to each member of his congregation, back out into the world once more, but now filled with the resilience of his sermon, his faith. *But in what?* Marta had recently found her mind revolting.

'Thank you, Father,' Marta mouthed as deliberately as she could when it was finally her turn to walk past him, all the time not losing sight of Mrs Kohler up ahead of her and now chatting to two ladies and a gentleman. She appeared to be alone. *Good, that was good. A husband would only want to talk less*, thought Marta, walking slowly out of church, carefully and yet self-consciously. Marta felt everyone's eyes pinned on her, watching her crude attempt to corner Mrs Kohler.

She continued to bide her time, watching her step on the disconnected stones winding through the churchyard and creating a pathway between the rows of gravestones and lifetimes, all here, peacefully recorded and on the surface, at quiet rest, before Marta rubbed a hand on one of her shoulders as a chill ghosted through.

Soon, sunshine broke out from behind a cloud overhead, washing the scene and buoying spirits and conversations gathered. The war was something to forget for one morning. A break in conversation up ahead, Marta's intuition spied. An opportunity Marta might have passed up in another life.

'Mrs Kohler?' Marta said, speaking a few feet away, to try and disarm her approach. 'How do you do? I am Mrs Richter… Meike's grandmother. She uses a wheelchair.'

'Yes.' Mrs Kohler paused, perhaps not meaning to come across as she did. 'I know who you are. I've seen your granddaughter. She seems lovely,' she said more softly. 'How may I help? And, please, it is Erna, Mrs Richter.'

Up close, Marta was privy to peer through the looking glass Mrs Kohler displayed to the rest of the world. She was sad, and Marta felt the pull of a connection.

'Mrs Kohler... Erna,' Marta said. 'I was hoping to speak with you privately, if we each had a few moments this morning. It is a little urgent and it's about Meike. She was taken... like Horst, your son, I believe.'

There, she had said it out loud. Silence for a moment between them.

'There is a cafe... not far,' Mrs Kohler said, lighting a cigarette and suddenly looking more hardened to life.

'Super... Erna,' Marta said awkwardly.

The pair of them walked away from their local church, both in short heels, kinder to calves of women reaching a certain age. Around them, Berlin bustled in a polite, Sunday morning fashion. As they walked and observed people and greetings and conversations, it felt like how a Sunday in Berlin used to, before, before all this, until they cast their gaze up and were brashly reminded by National Socialism flags decorating every street. How could it be like before? Mrs Kohler then blindsided her beautifully, articulating so simply what Marta's mind had failed to all this time.

'How did we let these monsters in?' she said, walking next to her and taking a draw from a cigarette. 'How stupid we were.' Lowering her face, she took a last puff of nicotine before stubbing it out beneath her heel with a movement at odds with her facade. A tear then caused her to tilt her head skyward like she could catch it before it fell. A quiet stream of them followed, rolling down her cheeks and stopping Marta in her tracks.

'Oh, Mrs Kohler! I am so sorry if I have upset you. Please...' said Marta.

Marta held Mrs Kohler with her arms and walked her down a side street, away from spying eyes. Mrs Kohler managed to stop herself, resting a hand flat across her breast like she was rebalancing her emotions, though her eyeliner, flawless moments earlier, was ruined. The pair of them stood in an alley, shadows of buildings reaching high around them. Up close, the sober lighting added a decade to Mrs Kohler's face. Marta tried not to notice the more pronounced wrinkles ageing her new acquaintance. At these quarters, Mrs Kohler was pungent of nicotine.

'No... Mrs Richter, you haven't upset me,' she said. 'You said his name... Horst. We don't say his name anymore. Mr Kohler, you understand, believes in moving forward. Chin chin and all that.'

Mrs Kohler lit another cigarette, which Marta thought in the moment was the last thing she needed, but she knew it was not her place to question, only to listen.

'Mr Kohler wrote to our doctor about a year ago. He wanted Horst – how can I put it? – euthanised... euthanised,' she said a second time in odd amusement, which Marta found unseating. 'Our son wasn't a pet.'

Marta stood still and listened to Mrs Kohler's words float towards her through puffs of smoke. A pause.

'Mr Kohler asked your doctor to have Horst killed?' Marta feared she had been too blunt.

'Yes. Our family physician refused. How would he not? He's a kind man... not like *them*,' she said, removing the last word from her lips like it was tar from her cigarette. 'That wasn't enough for Walter.' She laughed. 'Of course not. He wouldn't let the matter drop, so he wrote to Hitler's private office with the proposition: it was kinder Horst *not* be allowed to live.'

Marta could not hide her feelings anymore. It was the response Mrs Kohler had been looking for all this time like a lost locket. She had not found it among her circle of friends.

A group of Berliners, talking loudly, walked past the end of the alley back out on the main boulevard, but they did not notice them. The warmth of their gaggle was soon followed once more by the coolness of the alley's shadows where they had sought refuge.

'Horst is dead, Mrs Richter,' Mrs Kohler said, fixing her face as if it was the only way she could get the words out.

What?! Marta's head exploded.

'He's dead. I received a letter from Hadamar, where they were keeping him... from influenza,' she quoted from memory. 'An abscess on his lung. The body had to be quickly cremated to avoid further infection. They offered me his ashes in an urn... at no cost.' She laughed like a sad drunk. 'How decent. What would I do with his ashes?' she said safely through the shield again of cigarette smoke.

An uncomfortable pause and Marta's eyes caught Mrs Kohler's before flicking down to her feet.

'What am I going to do, Mrs Richter?' she said.

25

It was mid-morning at the hospital. People were happy. Almost. Devil No.1 had just finished his rounds for another day. Relief, relative freedom. Ingrid and Meike's inspections had passed without incident, but a girl of rag and bones was brought in halfway through the morning's rounds and presented to the patients on the ward.

'This idiot slept outside last night,' Devil No.1 said, the girl buckling next to him with only a nightshirt on above blue knees like bolts. 'She has surprised me. The rest of you should thank her for her courage and efforts. Proud German soldiers are dying of exposure fighting right now in the East. This girl survived outside last night in only a nightshirt... in temperatures of ten below. I intend to write and inform Reichsführer Himmler himself.'

Meike, Ingrid and the rest of the patients remained perfectly still while they listened, like the doctor's words were a loaded revolver to their head. Heads bowed slightly, subservient. Each patient had been glad of the distance between them and *him*, Devil No.1, though Meike's heart broke for the sad girl stood beside the doctor.

Ingrid and Meike had exchanged glances from the

edges of their eyes. Angel No.1 noticed, gripping one of her hands in tension, which in turn caught the expert attention of Devil No.2. The kind nurse was willing the doctor to stop speaking, be done with this show, this whatever it was. Angel No.1 could not bear the girl's suffering and instead, to try and distract her brain, she studied the doctor's features, his slack mouth as it opened in different shapes, which in moments made his face appear completely round. She wondered why someone so richly indulgent in food and drink had perfect skin.

Devil No.1 finally, thankfully marched off, quickly followed by the other nurses led by Devil No.2. The kind nurse was last to leave, cue an outbreak of teenage chatter from all of the patients on the ward as the double doors swung closed behind her. Meike pushed across the ward to the girl who had slept outside all night, holding her hand and her eyes in hers as kindly as she could from her position below. On bare, knuckled feet, the girl seemed to be balanced like a tightrope walker. It looked painful, Meike could only wonder.

Ingrid watched Meike comfort the girl and in the moment, she only admired her, and more. She envied her, her humanity, Ingrid regretted, before remembering herself and finally abandoning standing duty and resting her aching legs. The girl who slept outside was ushered softly into bed by Meike and by the others. They covered her in bedding and rubbed her body all over to try and thaw her icy limbs as best they could.

'Horst has not gone home,' Ingrid later said to a disbelieving Meike and a circle of listening patients. 'He was in no state. Why discharge him when he was worse?'

'Ingrid, he's gone home,' Meike said. 'His parents must have contacted the hospital... and they agreed to let him leave. Where else has he gone?'

'Exactly,' Ingrid said.

'There's another ward here, a bad ward, on the other side of the hospital,' said another girl with a growth on one side of her face, as if it was pulling her head one way, but the rest of her face was still to catch up. Meike was captivated by her beauty. 'Maybe Horst is there.'

'A bad ward?' said Meike, refocusing on the discussion. 'What do you mean? A bad ward?'

'Devil No.1 and No.2 are capable of anything. Don't you get it yet, Meike?' said Ingrid and Meike felt affronted.

'Ladies... gentlemen,' the kind nurse interrupted. 'Your chores, your chores,' she said, clapping her hands briskly. 'Meike, that means you too.'

It was the following day and Meike was being weighed again by the kind nurse back in Devil No.2's office. Weigh-ins for each patient had increased from once to twice a week, which only made Meike feel like she was being watched more closely. She did not like the idea. Outside, the morning sky was a beautiful blue washed with early winter sun, rising and warming the atmosphere.

Behind Hadamar's bricks and mortar, Meike couldn't feel the sun on her skin, which frustrated her. She remembered spending time outside with her father and them both marvelling at how warm the sun was, the closest star to Earth and yet millions of kilometres away. In those moments, Meike's awe was impossibly caught between the magic of science and the magic of her father.

Meike blinked away the memory. At least in Devil No. 2's office, away from the main ward, she was free of the nausea of bleach constantly invading her senses. Her focus turned to the head nurse's desk, today all tidy and correct. No papers unattended.

'Come, Meike, let's weigh you, shall we?' the kind nurse said, pushing her in her chair up and onto the scales before turning away to play with the weights to achieve the correct balance.

'How are you feeling today, Meike? How's your stomach?' she said, taking the chance to fill the pause between them.

'Not bad today, thank you. Could be better... could be worse,' she said, distracted by a shadow dancing on the far wall. Devil No.2 hadn't taken down her Christmas cards, which now look tired and unloved. One was reflecting a bird feeder hanging outside. The feeder had attracted a robin, Meike recognised, turning around to check over her shoulder before her movement scared it off.

'Meike, you're still losing weight,' the kind nurse said. 'Look at you... skin and bone.'

But Meike wasn't listening. She said, 'What does "400 idiots x 5,000 reichsmarks = 2 million reichsmarks per year" mean?'

'What?' said the kind nurse.

'What does "400 idiots x 5,000 reichsmarks = 2 million reichsmarks per year" mean?' Meike said. 'I read it on some papers, left on the desk in here the other day.'

'You shouldn't have done that,' the kind nurse said.

'But I did,' Meike said with a rare tone. 'What does it mean?' she said before answering her own question. 'I think *we* are the idiots… you know how the doctor treats us… on his rounds. You see him every day.'

'What do you mean, Meike?' the kind nurse said, avoiding Meike's point. 'Oh, you are in a funny mood today. How can you be idiots? You're all just…' she said, searching for the right word, 'just… different… that is all. We all have our problems, Meike… even the doctor,' she said, glad to be able to tidy things back in their place and not have to confront the conversation directly. 'Your problem, young lady,' the kind nurse said, regaining some warmth, 'is you think too much. Concentrate on getting your weight back up and on your chores each day, Meike. This war will be over soon. Then we can all go home, and life can go back to normal.'

Meike mentally frowned as the kind nurse wheeled her off the crude hospital scales and began pushing Meike back out onto the ward, her patient's words playing in her head on repeat, like an itch she couldn't reach, for the rest of her shift.

26

It was early evening and Marta, Hans and Anselma were each seating themselves at their table to eat supper. Chicken cuts, roasted vegetables and a thin stock Marta had worked carefully to thicken as best she could with what was left in the pantry, ahead of ration day, this afternoon. Its earthy smell now rising from the table was comforting and lifted everyone's quiet mood. Anselma had spent today securely tucked away in her room, which caused Marta to complain to Hans as she peeled potatoes.

'Marta,' Hans said, 'she's still a teenager. What do you expect?'

'She's nineteen,' Marta answered. 'She's a young woman. She should be out... among people.'

Together, the three of them now each picked up a soup spoon accompanied by a supporting fork, and almost in unison and they began juggling hot potato in their mouths. Hans looked down at his bowl and he wished he had more meat, focusing on the meagre leg swimming lonely in the middle of his supper. Still, fresh meat was hard to find in Berlin as more and more of the country's food was shipped to the soldiers fighting on the fronts in the East and West.

'Yesterday, did you go anywhere particular, Anselma?' Marta asked as politely as she could between mouthfuls. She had lost her appetite rather, following a glass and a half of schnapps while preparing this evening's supper.

'I had LGG,' she said.

The League of German Girls, Marta's head translated, nodding thinly in reply.

'Do you have to spend so much time there?' she said.

'Yes, Grandma. All the girls at school go. Those who don't—'

But Marta snapped, 'I don't like it, Anselma. Your father taught you to think for yourself... you know he did.'

Hans breathed a sigh and closed his eyes. *Could they not just enjoy one, simple supper together?*

'Leave the girl alone, Marta,' Hans said. 'It's... just boys and girls... being boys and girls.'

'Thanks, Grandpapa,' Anselma said with a tone. 'And I'm nineteen, Grandpapa.' She laughed. 'I'm old enough to marry... and old enough to think for myself, Grandmother,' she said, losing any lightness in her words. 'I think the Party has some very good ideas about society. We need to help ourselves... as Germans, Grandmother. Why should Jews come here and eat our food and pollute our race?'

Marta held her breath. 'Pollute?' she said, shooting sharp eyes at Hans, who did not know how he could not be good cop in this conversation. 'What are you talking about, Anselma?'

'What were you doing at LGG yesterday?' Hans tried,

as casually as he could and returning wide eyes, discreetly, back across the table at Marta.

'We went out into the fields, Grandpapa, picking vegetables to feed our soldiers... feed *us*, Grandmother,' she said.

Picking vegetables, Marta's imagination scoffed.

Hans nodded, eternally grateful for an everyday exchange. 'Anything else?'

'We sang, Grandpapa,' she said. 'Our choir might be selected to sing at a Party rally in Nuremberg... I think next month.'

Without invitation, Anselma began to sing proudly. Out of tune. She never had anything approaching Meike's voice, Marta was painfully reminded now. Anselma sang:

'On its red and white background. Shines our black swastika bright.

'Victory sounds are heard all over, as the morning light breaks through.

'National Socialism. Is the future of Germany,' she finished.

'Beautiful,' Hans said, clapping warmly.

'Thank you, Grandpapa,' she said, bowing her head playfully.

But Marta could no longer contain herself. 'Spare a thought for your sister as you're singing with your friends,' she said, and Hans glowered at her. *That's not fair.*

'Marta, that's not the girl's fault,' he said, as if Anselma was not present at the table.

'No,' said Marta.

It was later in the evening and a part of Marta was still upset, washing up their supper dishes at their sink, wrist deep in murky water. The smell of chicken and vegetables emanated from their plates as she cleaned them. Hans dutifully stood alongside her, waiting to dry plates as Marta passed the first over, refusing to look in his direction as she did. A philosophical scoff from Hans.

'Anselma isn't doing anything wrong, Marta,' he said. 'All the girls at her school are in the LGG... what is she supposed to do? She's never been as brave as Meike. She never has.'

'No... she hasn't,' Marta said, handing Hans another soaked plate. 'That doesn't make anything that's happening now right, does it? Does it?' she repeated loudly.

Hans knew a row was only a comment away before a creek of a chair coming from their dining room postponed it for the moment. Anselma.

'Keep your voice down,' Hans hushed. 'She can hear us.'

Marta returned her eyes to the sink, frustrated, wearied. She gathered herself one last time for tonight. 'I am worried, Hans,' she whispered. 'Why doesn't she miss Meike more? It's her sister... her *sister*. Why doesn't she?'

'Of course she misses her,' Hans said, checking over his shoulder at the kitchen doorway. 'But she's nineteen, Marta... she's living life... her life. Everything is just starting for her. Even the National Socialists must seem exciting to her. She's allowed to be excited, Marta.'

'Yes,' Marta said, unconvinced.

'Go and sit down in the living room,' Marta said. 'I can finish in here. I'll bring you through a nightcap... catch up on your paper, Hans,' she offered with a dismissive hand, which Hans did not wholly appreciate, but he wasn't about to pass up peace and quiet, not presently. 'Go… go!' Marta tried to smile in the best apology he was going to get, before turning her back on him and allowing any pretence of joy to immediately fall from her face. 'I'll be through in a minute. There is something I want to tell you.'

Hans closed his eyes and tried to breathe quietly. Of course. There had to be a catch.

27

Oh no, the kind nurse panicked, her head a whirl like she had drunk her wine too quickly before eating. She was in Devil No.2's office and she knew she should not be. *Ouch*. A thin slice on her finger, a paper cut from rushing through piles of documents she knew were none of her business.

A typewriter anchored the centre of the head nurse's desk. A photograph, cheaply framed, which the kind nurse could not resist picking up and inspecting. A family portrait, with Devil No.2's husband, presumably, in full military uniform alongside three children in Hitler Youth dress. Everyone wore serious faces, posed in a pristine garden of what would have otherwise been a pretty rural home. She had never seen the head nurse wearing anything other than her Hadamar uniform before. A flurry of a bird outside the office window and the kind nurse was grateful to be reminded where she was: somewhere she shouldn't be. *It has to be here somewhere, it has to be.*

Papers, overlooked by the Nazi eagle imperious at their top, all seeing, always watching and heading a document containing an uninviting maze of words and numbers.

'A patient consumes on average 700 grams of marmalade a month,' the kind nurse read. 'One kilo of marmalade costs 120 reichsmarks, meaning 5,903,000 kilos of marmalade are saved, equating to 7,083,500 reichsmarks over ten years.'

What? the kind nurse thought, holding the paper up now in her hand, like its contents would become clearer in the light. Hadamar had run out of marmalade months ago. None now seemed forthcoming for patients to enjoy with their breakfast each morning. The kind nurse assumed it was due to simple food shortages, stores being diverted to the front.

'How dare you?' A voice behind her. 'What is the meaning of this?'

Oh no. Angel No.1 turned around with dread and faced her fear.

'I am so sorry, Head Nurse, for the intrusion. I thought a patient may have left something in here after being weighed yesterday.'

'Lost something?' the head nurse said tightly. 'What do you care if they lost something?'

'Of course, Head Nurse. I will return to my duties at once… at once,' she said, head bowed submissively to avoid further scrutiny. The head nurse held her lips as the kind nurse made her way uncomfortably past. Too close for comfort, as Angel no.1 was almost free.

'They are lumps of flesh,' the head nurse said behind her, halting the kind nurse where she stood as if the words were magnetised. 'Lumps of flesh, that is all. Worthless, useless, idiots, all of them, serving no purpose, of no value.'

The kind nurse listened, unmoving, before lifting her head up slowly to look directly at Devil No.2. She could not believe that she was being brave enough to study her features briefly. She was always so keen to escape those eyes. Hadamar's head nurse stared at her, without any feeling the kind nurse could easily read.

'What do you suppose we are doing here, Miss Weber?' Devil No.2 said.

'Caring for the sick?' The kind nurse could no longer maintain eye contact and turned her face down once more to the floor.

'We have not got time to care, Miss Weber. There is too much to be done… to be achieved.'

'Of course, Head Nurse,' the kind nurse said without thought. 'Absolutely, we are very busy at the moment preparing for next week's visit from Reichsführer Himmler's office. We are honoured to be receiving such guests,' she said, turning around again in a renewed bid to leave the confrontation. Her body felt locked in purgatory.

'Oh… and Miss Weber,' Devil No.2 said, making the kind nurse turn back to face her once more. 'Don't let me ever catch you in here again.'

'Yes,' the kind nurse said hurriedly, before pacing back out onto the hospital corridor.

28

Marta paced into their living room to find her husband, Hans, who she knew would be sat reading and enjoying his newspaper. He quickly looked up and sensed her haste, closing the newspaper and placing it down on their coffee table. Before she could speak, she was hit by a smell in the room.

'Have you been smoking?' she said, breaking her train of thought. 'Oh... it doesn't matter,' answering her own question.

She took a seat opposite her husband while continuing to dry her hands on a tea towel. They were wet from washing this evening's supper plates at their kitchen sink. Hans leant forward slightly and looked at her, listening.

'I spoke to Mrs Kohler after church on Sunday,' Marta said. 'The mother of a boy who was taken into hospital... like Meike was.'

'Okay,' said Hans, trying to prevent any escalation of emotion.

Finally, Marta put down her tea towel and concentrated. 'A lovely lady... very elegant. She – Mrs Kohler,' Marta corrected herself, 'is upset, Hans, upset at what happened to Horst... to her son. You remember him from church? He walked peculiar, part of his condition, I remember Meike once explaining to me.'

'I don't.' Hans shook his head unhelpfully and Marta worked to contain her frustration.

'She has received a letter from the hospital where Horst was a patient. Hans... her son is dead. He's dead.'

Hans's mind felt it must have missed something.

'I don't understand, Marta,' he said. 'The boy had a condition... since birth. Was that right? It cut his life very short. What does that have to do with Meike? She is very different, you know that. She had an accident,' he said as his wife's face skewed in resistance to information she already well knew.

'What does it have to do with Meike?' Marta whispered angrily. 'It has everything to do with Meike, Hans, everything.'

A pause between them both as Marta thought Hans might say something, but he didn't.

'They were both taken at home, Hans, against family wishes,' Marta continued in a hush. 'And now a boy is dead, Hans. Horst was not ill. He had a condition. He should have lived... for years... a happy life, like Meike.'

'We don't know that, Marta,' Hans said, sitting up in his armchair to avoid having to project his voice any further than he had to. 'That condition could have weakened him in all manner of ways. Children and people die, Marta... all the time. The things I saw in the war...' Hans finished, but letting his voice trail off. He knew what he had left himself open to.

'The war, the war,' Marta said, impatiently picking back up the tea towel she had placed down. 'Always the war,' she said. 'Something is wrong, Hans! The war is an excuse. What does anything have to do with poor Meike? What difference does it make… whether she is here now living with us, her grandparents, or in hospital… we don't know where? The bloody Party already has her poor father… Abbe…' But she had begun to bluster crassly and Hans never liked to hear it from a woman.

A light from the kitchen, radiating into the room's doorway, made both Hans and Marta's heads turn towards it. Anselma had come downstairs and was clinking in the pantry for a glass of milk before she went to bed. Hans and Marta turned back to face one another anew, but with no words now, only emotions running through their eyes like a river running high after rainfall.

29

'Hello, Doctor,' Marta said, trying not to sound hurried.

'Hello, Mrs Richter,' Dr Jung said from behind his desk, sporting a stethoscope loose around his neck.

Outside, the thin sky was grey and inky pale. Marta wasn't sure which way the weather would turn when she had looked up with a frown and left the house earlier. Meike had appeared in her mind.

'How can I help?' Dr Jung said, bringing her back to the room, happy to speak to a patient he knew well; less small talk.

'I am not here for myself, Doctor,' Marta said.

'Ah,' Dr Jung said and immediately shuffled in his chair as the parameters of the conversation had changed. Marta noticed, quietly, crow's feet sketching themselves gently from the corner of Dr Jung's eyes.

'I have discovered more information, Doctor, if I may... not perhaps directly relevant to Meike, but... significant, I hope you will agree,' said Marta, not yet ready to look her guest from the previous evening in the eye.

'I spoke with Mrs Kohler after church on Sunday.

Lovely lady... very elegant,' Marta said, pausing for a moment. 'Her son, Horst, was taken from their home, against her wishes, into hospital... Hadamar, I believe, as you said, not far from Berlin, only a few kilometres north of the city.'

'Yes, I know Hadamar,' Dr Jung said. 'It was an asylum of sorts for soldiers with diseased minds... shellshock, after the first Great War. Terrible condition... well, I know you... Hans.'

'I didn't know that, Doctor,' Marta said, and Dr Jung regretted reaching a wrong assumption. 'I guess Hans was lucky that he wasn't injured in the war.'

'Mrs Richter, I think everyone who fought in 1914 was injured, whether, as doctors, we were able to see their injuries or otherwise. It opened our eyes to that. And, for that, we should be grateful. But here we are again, aren't we?' he said, and Marta nodded softly.

She said, 'Do you know the name Schuster? A Dr Heinz Schuster? It was the signatory at the bottom of a letter Mrs Kohler received from Hadamar hospital, informing her that Horst, her son, had died.'

'Horst died?' the doctor said, more in confirmation than in question. 'I am... sorry to hear that. He was a polite young man.'

There was silence for a moment.

'May I ask, how did he die, Mrs Richter?'

'Influenza, an abscess on his lung,' Marta relayed from memory, from the letter she had been privy to.

'Thank you for telling me. I will know to be aware and to pass on my condolences when I next see Mrs Kohler. And Mr Kohler, of course.'

'The signatory at the bottom of the letter,' Marta said. 'Does the name Schuster ring a bell with you at all?'

Dr Jung breathed and cast his eyes higher into the room. It didn't, which concerned him, because nearly everyone knew everyone, at the very least by name, in medicine in Berlin.

'I don't, Mrs Richter, I'm afraid,' he said finally. 'And I am surprised that I don't, given that he must be quite senior. But, as we did discuss at your home the other evening, I am rather out of the loop these days. I am speculating, but perhaps he was appointed from outside of Berlin. You almost hope we lose the war again, don't you?' Dr Jung then said, happily surprising Marta with such frankness.

'I don't know, Doctor,' said Marta. 'We lost in 1918, didn't we?'

Dr Jung smiled and nodded. 'You are quite right, Mrs Richter,' he said. 'You are quite right.'

Marta was back walking outside, heading home again and trying not to contemplate what lay waiting for her there when she arrived. She felt peaceful. Looking up, the previously patchwork sky had melted into undisturbed blue, like the world's oceans were upside down, and Marta wished she could swim in their serene waters.

'Alfred,' Marta said with a start, almost walking into him close to the doctor's surgery. 'Alfred,' she repeated more calmly, 'lovely to see you. How have you been?'

'Fine… thank you, Mrs Richter,' he said before an uncomfortable silence hung between them.

'I hear, Alfred, you're an excellent football player,' Matra tried, keeping the conversation light, and Alfred began a smile and nodded modestly. A lady walked too closely by, brushing Marta, who moved closer to the side of the pavement where they stood stilted. Alfred mirrored her movement, but remained muted, and Marta felt her peace from a few moments earlier dropping into sadness. They both felt Meike's absence like a bruise.

'Could I buy you a cup of coffee, Alfred?' Marta said and Alfred, who was rapidly approaching Hans's lofty height, nodded. He felt closer to Meike in the company of her grandmother and the sensation was both comforting and pained in the same heartbeat. He had no prior life experience of emotional conflict. He felt overwhelmed.

They were sitting and glad of the simple, physical task of drinking coffee in squinting Berlin sunshine. Chatter and cafe life dancing all around them, at polar odds with their table's quietness, but also somehow in keeping. *Was there anything left to fear?* Alfred wondered, with a feeling he might have previously pigeonholed as happiness, but it was as if that true anchor had escaped him ashore and now he was alone, adrift at sea.

'We still don't know anything about where Meike is,' Marta said, placing her coffee back down on the table. She watched Alfred take in her words but fail to offer any in reply. 'How is school, Alfred?' she asked, steering again to gentler waters. 'Do raid sirens disturb your lessons during the day? I assume they must.'

'Yes, they do,' he said, failing to subdue the start of a smile. 'It's good if it's a lesson you don't like. But if it's a lesson you like…'

'And what lessons do you like, Alfred?' Marta asked, not about to refuse the obvious opportunity.

'German... and history.'

'Ahhhh... humanities. And a historian,' Marta said. 'A fine combination. We need more young men like you, Alfred. Do you know what you would like to do when you are older?'

A small shake of the head and Marta feared she had lost him once more before he said, 'I feel angry when I hear about injustice... I want people to know the truth.'

Marta smiled quietly and nodded.

'More coffee?' a waitress interrupted, poised to pour. 'Madam?' But Marta shook her head. 'Sir?' she added. Alfred blushed awkwardly and instinctively followed Marta's lead and shook his head also. The waitress left them alone again.

'She called you sir, Alfred,' Marta said with a smile, which was reciprocated as they both rose from their seats and Marta enjoyed the moment between them. She dipped into her purse, from her handbag, and left money on their table, underneath her napkin. Alfred immediately wanted to thank her, but he didn't, and he right away regretted not being brave enough to do so.

The pair of them made an unlikely couple as they left the cafe behind them and strolled along the high street in the northern quarter of the capital. Brilliant sunshine, in the afternoon, blinkered their vision. Laughter close by hugged them. It was Friday, the promise of a weekend. The smell of meat from a butchers, as Marta and Alfred passed outside, closing down for the day after a dawn start. Fumes of caffeine and tobacco rising above new cafe-goers, sitting and reflecting on another Berlin working week. National Socialism was good, or, it wasn't bad? Marta felt a shiver of guilt for being seduced for a moment.

'Alfred,' she said, putting her hand out to invite him to stop walking for a moment. Their homes were close. 'I'm so sorry you had to experience that... the night you visited Meike. I am not applauding, mind, your attempt to steal my granddaughter,' she added in happy reprimand. 'But... you didn't deserve to see that.' But her enthusiasm for sharing was suddenly waning. 'I wish...'

Too much information.

'It's fine,' Alfred said, in a shock of maturity in miniature, which Marta was realising he made a habit of. She could picture why Meike would like him. 'It's not your fault,' Alfred said with a sadness.

Marta looked at him, and she realised something deeper – he had been torturing himself too.

'Boys bully others at school... the ones who don't have any friends... who can't play football... sit at the front in class. *They'll put you on the bus to Hadamar*, they shout. Then they either cut their throat with their fingers or pretend they're choking. Everyone knows, Mrs Richter. It's no secret,' he said.

Everyone knows! Marta's mind ballooned. *Everyone knows what?!*

30

Five... no, six, yes, six, Alfred counted in his head in the black, which was slowly beginning to soften to his eyes. *Blast*, he thought. He had lost count. *Focus, Alfred*, he urged himself through clenched fists. *Eight... nine*. This was it. He could make out the shape of a door ahead on his right. Meike's room. He glanced over his shoulder, trying to ground himself as best he could, standing in this bleakness. *Why wasn't the darkness softening more?* He could hear someone moving behind the corridor wall, but out here they seemed unreachable to him and yet only this wall separated them. *Ten. Ten*, Alfred repeated in his head. Then chaos.

'Alfred? Alfred? Alfred!' his mother repeated, now appearing glaringly at the door, ajar, to his room. 'It's not like you to sleep in the day. You have a caller, Mrs Richter from across the street. She would like to talk to you,' his mother said, words pinched by anxiety.

'Hello, Mrs Richter,' Alfred said, greeting her at their front door.

'Invite Mrs Richter in, Alfred,' his mother said from

behind them, making Alfred cringe. 'Don't leave her standing outside.'

'No matter, Mrs Reis,' Marta said, saving Alfred from further embarrassment. 'I am unable to stop, I am afraid. I was simply hoping Alfred may like to come with Mr Richter and I to visit our granddaughter in hospital. If you are happy for him to, of course. She has a handicap,' Marta said, playing the guilt card and then quickly realising that Meike would have been annoyed with her for doing so.

'*I am me before anything else, Grandma,*' she imagined Meike reprimanding her, low by her side. '*And it's not sad, Grandma! I'm quite happy.*'

'*Of course, of course, dear,*' she always responded, and in her mind, she walked over to her granddaughter and she embraced her like she was the only other person in the world.

Marta's eyes returned to Alfred, standing in front of her. She felt the cold from outside clash with the warm air from inside the Reis' generous home. Alfred had been born into relatively good fortune.

'Come... come in, Mrs Richter,' Alfred's mother then fussed, closing their front door to the cold. 'Alfred?' she said. 'Would you like to go with Mr and Mrs Richter to visit their handicapped daughter in hospital?'

Marta's heckles immediately prickled at the word handicapped, like Alfred's mother had used it without permission first.

'*You see?*' Meike's ghost teased Marta.

'Yes... yes, I would like to go, Mother,' Alfred said.

'If that is alright with Mr and Mrs Richter,' his mother reminded him.

'Of course, Mrs Reis,' said Marta. 'It would mean a lot to my granddaughter.'

'Of course... very well,' Alfred's mother said and with that her son began to pull on the arms of his coat and his shoes on his feet, and he was out the front door, waiting for Marta to then prise herself free of his mother. Finally, she walked forward to Alfred, breaking out into a smile with mischief in her eyes. They were in cahoots. Given even everything, it felt like fun.

'We are going to Hadamar, Alfred,' Marta said. 'Are you ready, Alfred?'

He nodded.

In his car, Hans drove the three of them out of Berlin's choke and to the city's rural edges, on their journey north to Hadamar hospital. The clean sun of a January morning became clouded by grey in the sky, which began to produce gentle snowfall, Alfred watched through the windowpane, sat looking out of the back of Hans's car, which felt colder than Siberia. He wished he'd brought a bigger coat. He breathed heavily in loud puffs to try and warm himself before wishing he hadn't drawn attention to himself from Marta and Hans sat in the vehicle's front seats.

'Are you warm enough, Alfred?' Marta asked, looking over her shoulder.

'I'm fine, Mrs Richter, thank you,' Alfred said without pause.

He looked back out his passenger window and he was mesmerised by the snowflakes, falling more heavily all around and blanketing everything in white. In the car, nobody spoke over the vehicle's guttural movement. The three of them stayed wrapped in their thoughts.

'We'll be lucky to make it back at this rate,' Hans finally said, weathered hands tight on the steering wheel and leaning his head forward warily to illustrate his point.

'We will,' said Marta. 'Come on, let's keep going. Nearly there,' she added, though, secretly, she was concerned too. *Like Hitler could control the weather now*, she thought, shaking her head at herself as much as *him*.

'You horrible little man,' she said out loud.

'I beg your pardon!' Hans said. In the back, Alfred furrowed his brow and pretended not to hear.

'I'm sorry, darling,' Marta hushed, conscious of their passenger seated behind them, and she reached her eyes and a hand across and she placed it on Hans's knee, resting it there for a time. 'Not you, my dear… never you,' she said, removing her hand. '*Him*… of course.'

Hans nodded, still not sure, but refusing to take his eyes off the road in front of them, which felt like it was quickly being swallowed by the white. *Soon, there will be nowhere left for us to go*, he thought. He squinted forward and hastily rubbed the windscreen clean, for what it was worth, with the back of his large hand. Then, outbuildings before them, coated in white. This was it.

'Would you like to wait in the car, Alfred?' Marta said, turning around. 'Just until we know we're in the right place.'

'Okay,' he said, and Hans could not help but frown to himself. His wife clearly had a relationship with this boy, this boy he did not know. He laid the concern to one side and looked across at his wife.

'Let's go,' she said, looking at him and Hans pursed his lips in agreement.

Alfred watched them walk up to the hospital, footsteps

sinking in the thickening snow. Now the warmth of the car engine was not running, it was becoming breathtakingly cold sat in the back seats. Alfred tried to hold himself somehow in an attempt to stay warm.

He peered out through the icy window. Snow was still falling heavily. Thin glass separated him from the army of flakes increasingly whipped by the wind and indiscernible, only a wall of white. Alfred shifted forward and tried to peer through the car's front windshield, but in the worsening conditions he could hardly make out the shell of the building ahead, being swallowed in the distance. He had forgotten its appearance from only a few minutes before and he cursed his memory for failing to recall it. He needed to know, but his eyes weighed heavy. He peered forward again, and he thought he saw a flicker of two figures for a moment, making their way up towards the building. Hans and Marta. But they were soon too small for Alfred to trace their movements. Sleep was coming on stronger, seducing him into unconscious.

He awoke with embarrassment, pulling his frame upright in the back of the car and immediately experiencing the cold once more, sat on the waxy leather.

'Why didn't you say something?' he heard Marta complain, loudly climbing into the front passenger seat. Hans breathed audibly and settled into the driver's seat as inconspicuously as he could. Alfred fixed himself perfectly still, like an involuntary voyeur to something seemingly very personal and private between two people who had shared a whole life together.

'She's in there,' Marta said through the start of a sob. 'She's in there, Hans… I know it.'

Alfred didn't dare say anything. It seemed unthinkable that he would do so, instead, bowing his head in the back and trying to block out the words confided in front of him. Marta then began to cry, buckling forward in her seat like she had a cramp in her stomach. Hans and Alfred were anguished to witness her pain. They wanted anything and everything but this. After a silence, Hans placed a large hand, skin like parchment, on Marta's back, although her sobs had already begun to subside. He began to speak, but he continued looking forward up to the building.

'You heard what they said, Marta,' Hans said. 'They're under orders to not let anyone in. They have good reason. They are doing their jobs. We are at war, remember... remember what that was like?'

Alfred was glad of Hans's words before Marta breathed. She said, 'Yes, Hans, but we're not at war here in Germany, are we? We're fighting in France, in Poland... in Russia... but not here in Germany. This was never our war, Hans, this is Hitler's war,' she said, turning her face angrily away from her husband. 'The way he made France surrender in the same train we surrendered in, in 1918. It's childish revenge... madness. Can't anyone see? If only some Tommy had done the decent thing in 1914 and blown his bloody brains out... stupid little man... none of this would be happening.'

Discomfort followed and the three of them sat still with their thoughts, Alfred longing suddenly to be back home, away from here, but he knew Meike's potential presence was holding Marta in this place like a moon in orbit. Alfred peered out his passenger window. A thick sky overhead was growing dusky. No snow picturesquely like before, just streaks of blackening sleet, creasing the weather around them.

31

It was the afternoon, and his walk today was feeling, for Alfred, like forever. At school, he hadn't been able to focus. The final lesson of the school day had been tortuous. The clock on the class wall seemed to tick backwards until it was finally, finally time and he could hurry out the gates and embark upon what he wanted to do today, head on foot to Hadamar, which he had travelled to by car with Hans and Marta. He had to see for himself.

The drive home from Hadamar with Meike's grandparents had proved unbearable, and Alfred had vowed in his head as he waved them politely farewell never to repeat the experience any time soon. Alfred knew he was stubborn, and he also was at least aware that it was both a strength and a flaw. Hadamar hospital: he *had* to see for himself. Little else had been able to occupy his mind this afternoon as, through the classroom windows, Alfred watched rainfall, which refused to relent. Like the clock hanging in the classroom, the rain appeared fixed on freeze frame as if it wasn't falling at all but, instead, suspended between clouds and concrete. Stuck like

Alfred's mood since Meike was taken, today mirrored that feeling. He had never felt like this before – sad.

A week earlier had been the same, Alfred's sixteenth birthday, a landmark for any young Berliner. Alfred's parents had looked so proud, beaming, but that perversely had only highlighted in Alfred's mind how low his emotions had sunk. He blew out candles on his cake and he looked up and he smiled vacantly at his mother, and yet none of it had meant anything. As if he had become an imposter in his own life. Standing over their kitchen table, filled generously with sweet treats his mother had lovingly baked, and with sugar she had been squirrelling away in the weeks leading up to the day, Alfred had wished so hard for Meike to be there. But she wasn't, instead, only appearing in his dreams at night, never clearly or within reach. *Ten, Alfred repeated in his head. Then chaos.*

Alfred cut now through flat fields dangerously laden with crops, dangerous because they were on the point of spoiling and going to waste, waste neither families at home across Germany nor soldiers fighting in the West or the East could afford. But who was left now to harvest them?

Alfred walked down thin paths bordering vast fields, like tiptoeing on the frame of a godly masterpiece. Rain started to fall heavy on his head, hurrying him to lift up the hood of his winter coat. Squelch. Alfred looked down and he saw one of his previously smart school shoes sunk in mud. His mother was going to go mad. *Oh no.* Splatters of brown, like flicks of paint, were creeping too up the bottom of his smart school trousers and making Alfred wince anew. Next time, he would remember. For today,

Alfred reached down and folded the bottom of his soiled trousers tightly into his socks.

He stood tall once more and the wind picked up and buffeted his face, forcing him to turn his head down against the elements as he continued to stride on. He couldn't have picked a worse afternoon if he had tried. He lifted his head to face the wind and the rural rain as if in surrender. He thought he was going to cry, but he didn't. Instead, in the middle of this wildness, Alfred felt something, something surprising. He felt alive.

Alfred's eyes were lit like matches, and he started to crack a smile. He raised his head and faced once more the slap of the wind against his cheeks, pushing his shoulders back and mock marching like a soldier in the German army, imagining Meike laughing out loud at how foolhardy he was for striking out on such a journey in this weather. In his mind, he smiled broadly back at her. He continued to stride boldly forward, walking across a ditch pooling quickly with rising rainwater, which, as Alfred looked skyward with a squint, seemed set like the weather gods were in no mood now to call a halt. The sodden mud beneath his feet pulled at the soles of his shoes like treacle with each sticky step forward. Alfred managed to hop across another ditch and finally, he was here, he had reached the straight road north out of Berlin. He had made it. This far. The road felt to Alfred like another living thing briefly. He paused and he looked around, completing a 360-degree circle of where he stood. All he could see were fields. Nothing for it but to keep pressing forward.

His motivation faltered momentarily as he felt the tug of home, collaring his conscience like when he was little and being called by his mother for supper. He toyed with the thought of turning home before deciding that, no, he would lie to his mother and tell her that he had lost track of time playing football with friends after school. His head began to do the maths and imagined his mother warning him of the dangers of not coming home immediately, given the late afternoon bombing raids by the British.

There it is. He instinctively recognised ahead a turn in the road, alone and innocuous, reaching into thick woods. It looked like a road to nowhere, one nearly all would easily pass, but Alfred knew what, or where, lay hidden within.

32

Meike awoke with a start and immediately realised she was in hospital. God had not even allowed her a blissful half second believing that she was warm and safe in bed at her grandparents' home. Instead, she opened her eyes to another day in Hadamar, another day in here that she had no choice but to face. Her eyes opened wide only to be startled by revulsion, the doctor, Devil No.1, smiling and leering with lust.

Meike recoiled as if she was faced with a slug, giant beyond all nightmares, sliding up her pristine bed. Because of her injury, she had no feeling below her waist and yet she could smell the doctor's hands reaching, pawing unwanted up gentle thighs. She tried to push him away with her arms and her hands, push away this horror, but it was little use. She looked up and there was Devil No.1's face, smiling.

'Meike.' A voice. 'Meike... Meike!' Again.

Meike opened her eyes and breathed out audibly, gratefully. Only the kind nurse's face was before her, rolling smiling eyes at the fact that she had fallen asleep after breakfast.

'Time to get you up, young lady,' she said, busily reaching around her and tidying up as much as she could while Devil No.2 was not on the ward. In the neighbouring bed, Ingrid was transferring into her chair in preparation for today's visit of the local LGG branch, the League of German Girls. Ingrid's legs, leaden like Meike's, spasmed angrily after being moved too roughly, pushing her chest back sharply where she sat. Ingrid weathered the jolt before ill-temperedly regaining control of her frame and quickly straightening her legs roughly beneath her like they were to blame. Meike watched her neighbour with a knowing smile and then noticed her pause her eyes oddly on her swollen ankles. Ingrid peered down at them with hate. She wished for pretty ankles, so that she could sit carefree outside in the summer back home in Switzerland. But her ankles were not pretty, no matter how long she allowed her eyes to linger upon their ugly, swollen shape. She blinked and imagined herself away from here for a few moments, her father growing cross with her as he watched her age too quickly into a woman.

'Ingrid! Sit still... and upright, by your bed,' a nurse said. 'They're here!' she hushed. 'The LGG will be on the ward any moment.'

33

Alfred curiously walked down a thin road flanked by tall trees. The trees reached high into the sky, making him feel like a little boy. As he walked, he found his hearing gradually tuning in, like his father's wireless, to his surroundings. The hum of the road ferrying traffic to and from Berlin behind him. The baseline of trees moving in the breeze beneath bright birdsong playing sharply all around. Mother nature's symphony. Alfred had never heard it so clearly.

Experiencing it, he realised now, had distracted him from how cold he was, the damp of the rain, which had relented here walking beneath the treetops, was wrapping around his bones like creepers. Alfred tilted his head upward and he tugged his hood off his head, feeling the freshness of the fading February light on his face. The wind was audible, moving overhead in a rhythm Alfred could not discern, but it was as if overhead spirits were guiding him and swaying even the tallest trees with its spectral push and pull. The movement of the trees was mesmerising, tilting at their tops in the ghostly elements, tipping this way and that like they each had a character of their own. Individual. Benign.

Alfred felt cold again, and he pulled his coat hood back tightly over his head. He looked forward. The arrowing road ahead appeared to reach a dead end, like it was making a statement of intent. The wind picked up again, its sound different and guttural like a warning. Alfred picked up his pace and walked faster and faster and faster until his breathing became heavy. Then, overhead, a large bird, a kite, stunning in crimson, glided elegantly. This was it.

The road concluded before him with a simple, wooden barrier, telling him tacitly to stop, go back. Go home. Then, out of the corner of his eye, a path appeared to Alfred's right, worn by footsteps treading down grass. *Their mistake.* The devil in Alfred smiled, and he took the path.

34

From the LGG, a gaggle of young women shuffled warily through the double doors, which ushered them onto a ward at Hadamar hospital. The further they ventured forward, the closer the circle they formed.

'Come... come, girls,' said the group's mistress, resplendent in her National Socialism uniform.

Next to Meike's bed, Ingrid looked up briefly and closed her eyes. It was difficult for her to watch girls who mirrored her friends from back home in Switzerland. Slim, pretty, blonde. On the group's fringes, a darker brunette.

Devil No.1 and No.2 paced slowly in front of the visiting party, wearing their best smiles. *They are so obvious*, thought Meike.

'The girls look splendid, just splendid,' Devil No.1 said to the LGG mistress, who smiled tightly in reply, while the young women behind them all giggled en bloc. 'Sister, please,' Devil No.1 said to Devil No.2.

Hadamar's chief nurse began speaking. 'Girls, welcome to the ward where patients are first committed here to Hadamar. If they are able to prove in here that they are strong and that they can contribute productively to the Third Reich, then they are free to leave us and re-enter society, where they will be ready and equipped to live fulfilling lives... despite their handicap.'

Ingrid muttered under her breath, which the kind nurse, standing nearby, heard and silently winced.

Devil No.2 continued speaking. 'Of course, patients from Hadamar may always need some level of care from the National Socialist state, throughout the course of their unfortunate life and yet, equally, some of our most shining triumphs can go on to live happy... normal lives. Some may even have children,' she said.

The young women from the LGG moved slowly forward behind her, continuing to hug the centre of the ward like an island surrounded by deep water. Meike looked on and caught a flash of a face, immediately making her flush with heat. *That's ridiculous*. It couldn't be.

Morning light washed in from the ward's high windows, painting a benign scene. Some of the LGG girls were disappointed to see that patients at Hadamar hospital looked remarkably normal, not dissimilar, God forbid, to them.

Meike fought to manage her breathing before looking back up at the group from the LGG, perfectly uniform, sporting perfect black skirts cut below the knee and perfect white blouses decorated with a black neckerchief displaying the National Socialist eagle. Another flicker of recognition. Flushes, more rapid now, rushed to Meike's head. *It couldn't be, it couldn't*, Meike raced to contemplate, confused and intoxicated all at once. She could not translate what was happening. The kind nurse spied her distress and tried to ignore it.

Meike lifted her head up once more and every other figure on the ward, whether patient or temporary visitor, blurred into the background, like heat shimmering in summer. All except one, unmistakable. Anselma. It *was* Anselma. Her sister. *My sister!*

'Anselma!' Meike wished she could cry out, yell, scream from the bottom of her lungs as she hitched her frame up as high as she could in her wheelchair. Straining, craning, every inch of her frame. Out of the corner of her eyes, the kind nurse watched Meike with rising aggravation. What was she doing? *Meike! Will you ever learn?*

Anselma.

Anselma.

Anselma, Meike's mind raced now like a rollercoaster, flooded with hope and happiness and light. Meike felt light. Home. She would be able to go home. She could go home, surely. *Surely*. It had all been a misunderstanding, yes, a terrible misunderstanding. Her sister, a member of the LGG, would explain. They would understand. How could they not understand?

The sensations rushing through Meike's body made her feel so heady that she felt she would lift up from the ward floor and float out of Hadamar like in a hot air balloon, Devil No.1 and No.2 left grasping, jumping at thin air beneath her as if she was the heroine in her own fairy tale.

Anselma! the voice in Meike's head cried out once more, but still silenced, muted by fear soaked into her bones since her very arrival at Hadamar. Why didn't her sister say something? *Say something Anselma. Say something!*

Helpless, Meike struggled to lift her body up higher and higher in her chair, as if she was trying to reach out of it, balanced by the flat of her palms, locked in tension on the top of her chair's two wheels. She tried once more to catch her sister's eye. *She can't miss me. How could she miss me? Any second.* Then, everything would be okay. Everything *was* okay. It was over. It was over. Meike was going home.

35

The kind nurse looked again across at Meike shuffling in her chair. *What is the matter?* Devil No.2 glanced across at them both, simmering herself with agitation. Devil No.1, meantime, continued sycophantically to make small talk with the LGG mistress, still smiling anonymously in reply. The girls from the LGG moved forward, nearer the ward's exit.

What? Meike's head exclaimed. *Why can't she see me? She must… have seen me. She must… what is happening?*

Meike's eyes burned at her sister's back, but Anselma was leaving, head bowed, chin tucked tightly into the top of her breast, eyes following the floor at her feet. She did not look up, did not look back as she slowly walked away to Meike's right, positioned safely inside the group she had arrived within only a short time before. And yet they both secretly felt a lifetime had passed between them. Her sister.

It was her big sister, who, when she was little, she looked longingly up to, whispering, giggling plans into her ear no one else was important enough in her world to hear. Anselma would translate Meike's messages to onlookers watching lovingly on, waiting on tenterhooks for glimpses into what was going on behind Meike's wide eyes. It was years before Meike found her own voice.

Anselma continued to walk forward, guilty steps closer to the ward's exit, desperate to open her stride and move faster than the rest of the group would allow, away from where her little sister now sat, unmoving, silent once more.

'Anselma,' Meike said softly, but no one close to her could be sure they had heard.

The girls from the LGG paused for half a step, momentarily uncertain. Devil No.2 span around to look squarely at Meike only to be met by a wail.

'Anselma!' Meike cried, like a wounded infant being abandoned by the herd's elders, left to face its fate out of sight. She could not be saved. Tension in the space tightened like a noose.

'Nurse! Silence this impertinence at once!' Devil No.2 ordered the kind nurse, flaming with embarrassment. 'At once, Nurse!'

Devil No.2 turned away and began offering profuse apologies to their guests, private apologies which were impossible to pick out unless you were very close. The girls took heed from Devil No.2's placatory tone and were ushered away by her words like an incantation until, finally, they were out of sight, leaving Meike and the other patients behind on the hospital ward, behind in their world the LGG had not known prior to today. Still did not know, not really, beneath bleached surfaces and smiles.

The kind nurse rushed to Meike, crouching low by her side as the other nurses looked on and shared knowing eyes.

'What is it, Meike? What is the matter?' she said, placing a hand on her arm. 'What were you thinking? You must be more careful, Meike,' she fussed without waiting for Meike's answer to her question.

'My sister,' Meike said, starting to sob, dropping her head into her hands. Tears wetted the back of the kind nurse's hands when she reached up to Meike's face. 'That was my sister,' Meike sobbed again.

The other patients closed their ears to Meike's cries, a pain they had all heard before. Appalled at Meike's statement, the kind nurse put a hand to her mouth, while the other patients, in perfected mannerisms, looked to the floor in resignation. They had hoped for a happy ending for Meike, but instead now they were witnessing what they always feared. She was no different, she was not special.

Ingrid remained silent, thinking of something to say, something, anything to interrupt the quiet which sounded like a cacophony. She began shaking her head.

'Jesus Christ,' she said finally. 'Her sister.'

36

Anselma tried to shake off the emotion she was experiencing after witnessing her sister at Hadamar. *Meike is better off in hospital*, she thought, *especially while Germany is at war. She was lucky. What did she have to worry about now? Her whole life was taken care of.*

One evening over supper, Anselma's grandmother had tried to casually drop into sparse conversation and ask her about her visit to Hadamar. They had barely spoken since. Anselma was still speaking to her grandfather, Hans, who had proudly fought for Germany in the first Great War. An Aryan man, which her father Abbe was not entirely. She pined for a different reality and life with her mother.

She looked down now at the food on her supper plate and pushed it around. Tired vegetables, chunks of cheap meat. Marta looked at her and felt bitter conflict was only a few words away. Hans sensed a fight re-brewing.

'What do your friends at the LGG say, Anselma?' Marta had tried as the two of them cleared plates from the table. An uncomfortable Hans shifted in his chair in the neighbouring room and struggled to focus on his newspaper. *To heck with it.* He was going to roll a cigarette. The ill feeling could not get much sourer around here. He luxuriously smoked most of it in his imagination while rolling the thin papers between long fingers.

'They don't know her, Grandma. Why would they talk about Meike?' Anselma said sharply.

'Not Meike, I know they don't know Meike,' Marta said. 'People your age… like her… in her position.'

A pause in speech. In the other room, Hans rushed final puffs of his cigarette, filling his head with a miniature flurry of intoxication. Even giving up, well, almost giving up, had its advantages.

'Spastics, you mean?' Anselma said bluntly and Marta had to hold her temper, like she was holding her breath. 'Who can't look after themselves properly… can't even control themselves in bed at night? It's disgusting.'

Marta breathed deeply. She could feel heat rushing to her cheeks as she made her way to the kitchen sink and quickly began filling it with soapy water ready to rinse tonight's supper plates. Anselma watched her and she hid a secret smile.

'How can you think of your sister like that?' Marta said, her back safely to her granddaughter. From her position over the sink, Marta slowed her splashing and she tried to listen intently as if it was possible to read her granddaughter's thoughts. 'Meike loves you,' Marta said, unable to listen any longer, but Anselma was already pacing upstairs.

Once in her room, she slumped on her bed and let out a loud huff. She wished she had it in her to cry easily.

In the following days, Anselma's head continued to flash uncomfortably with images from her visit to

Hadamar. Her sister. Calling her name out loud. Lying to the other LGG girls on the bus ride back to Berlin. Their visit had begun so innocently before reaching what the doctor, who led their tour, called Hadamar's 'starvation ward' and marked the final stop of their visit.

'Come, come,' the doctor had invited with wide-eyed enthusiasm. Even the LGG mistress had hesitated. 'This is the reason I wanted you to see our little hospital and its inhabitants. It is a message from our Führer himself. A message that *his* is the way forward… it is the future, girls… the future of the Third Reich. The beginning of the next 1,000 years. Heil Hitler,' he added.

On the starvation ward, double doors ballooned open into initial darkness before eyes had time to adjust to the shadows. Heavy drapes were erected crudely across windows, with sunlight only seeping in through the cracks. Quiet whimpers were not frightening at first.

'Come, come!' the doctor hushed like it was early Christmas morning, eyes alight in the dusk. 'Don't be shy, girls. This is the home of the bottom of society, chunks of meat which are beyond feasting. Their final use is reminding us that *we* are on the right path.'

It was too much, but the doctor continued speaking before anyone could interrupt.

'Our Führer and Propaganda Minister Goebbels tell us in their broadcasts each evening that there is only room in Germany for pure Aryans. Pure of body and mind. Here at Hadamar, we are witnessing the last of inbreds, fit only for our history books, girls.'

Anselma wasn't listening. She looked down where she stood, with no interest to lift her gaze, but her eyes fought her as they grew accustomed to the darkness, acting like a barrier between them and the patients.

'Come, girls,' the LGG mistress ushered, with a handkerchief in one hand never far from her mouth. The group walked forward tightly. At its edges, Anselma at least now was unafraid to stray. Unlike the others, she at least knew that Meike wasn't infectious. The only contagion here was fear.

Anselma looked to her left at what she thought was a girl, although she couldn't actually be certain. The patient sat calmly at the end of her well-made bed could have been fifteen or fifty. They appeared to have no nose, only spots of nostrils where one should be, making Anselma's instincts flinch and take half a step back.

They suddenly caught each other's eyes, which Anselma instinctively shied from and was transfixed by in the same breath. The patient shifted their gaze away before turning it back to Anselma. The darkness felt oddly dry. The patient was fully clothed bar bare feet, buckled in from their big toe and craggy like an old woman's. Perhaps she *was* a girl and more like Anselma than either wished to recognise. A girl from the LGG then shrieked and grabbed a friend for dear life before giggles of relief from the rest of the group. A boy, undoubtedly this time, not very old, hung ragged in pyjamas which looked like they had not left his frame for months. He was hugging a mop head on the floor like it was a perverse lover, licking what moisture he could from its fingers.

'Why is he doing that, Mistress?' one of the girls asked and there was a relief for everyone in the spoken word. The LGG mistress looked across to the doctor, only too happy to answer.

'In these final acts, these youngsters are able to provide a service to the Reich,' he said. 'They can tell us how long a human can survive without food… water. They reveal to us the body's limits when exposed to severe cold, like our brave soldiers currently fighting the Slavic menace on the eastern front. Patients here on this ward regularly sleep outside… particularly in winter when we can be sure of ideal conditions. Take this girl here,' the doctor said, reaching full flow and holding out a hand like she was an entree at a restaurant. 'She slept outside last night in only her nightwear in conditions of minus ten Celsius.'

The group peered forward, almost as one, studying the girl more closely as she shivered tightly in the foetal position beneath a thin sheet, which looked in no way equipped to warm her again. No one spoke as the girl's teeth chattered in the silence. A pale, bare foot, too big for stick-like legs, stuck out from beneath the sheet. The girl's eyes were sunk back in her head, while her mouth was half open like she was frozen alive, or dead. She was unthreatening.

A girl from the group stepped forward to drink her in with her eyes before then moving on and paying her no further attention. With both his hands, the doctor pushed open the double doors at the end of the ward for the group and was soon followed by the LGG mistress, glancing over her shoulder to ensure her pupils were close behind.

Anselma combed her hair behind her ears and blinked in recognition of where she now was, safe and warm and fed. Cared for, in the luxury of her grandparents' suburban Berlin home. Her conscience shrugged. She could not picture her sister in Hadamar, where the starvation ward perhaps one day awaited her. At least her jealousy of Meike's nose, petite and pretty like their mother's, was fading, she considered as she ran a finger thoughtfully down the long nose she had inherited from her father. *Abbe*, her imagination sounded, like it was the most ridiculous name. *If only they knew*, she thought, sitting up in bed, *Meike was in Hadamar*. Her grandmother was right.

'Stupid cow,' she said out loud.

37

Almost every day, Alfred completed his pilgrimage to Hadamar after school. To hide his trips, he would lie to his mother that he had football practice with the school team. Alfred was not convinced his mother believed him, but he was still waiting for her to challenge him on what he considered a small deceit.

He could not shake a weight of sadness, which he carried like a satchel on his back. But when he was alone late each afternoon, in the expansive countryside north of the city's limits, the sense of relief he experienced each time took his breath away, like the satchel on his back lifted in these moments when only the rural fields invited him forward, each step sowed with the tiny hope that today might be the day – the day he discovered Meike.

Alfred could inform her grandparents of her whereabouts, even perhaps his own parents. Then the matter would be settled, surely. *Surely*. Meike would return home. It had all been a simple administrative error, by a Party bureaucrat who had never known a Meike Richter, never cared to consider her. Alfred knew Meike used a wheelchair, of course, and he instinctively sensed that her legs did not work, but they had never discussed it. It was unspoken between them, like the happy hesitation before a first kiss. No need for words, complicating uncertain perfection.

Overhead, a sky hung grey. Its mood was not encouraging Alfred to complete the journey on foot to Hadamar and yet, as ever, he was grateful he had once en route. Looking up and filled with the energy of his trip, the grey and its complex beauty was more compelling to him than perfect blue. Those brilliant skies felt oddly flat now. Alfred felt trapped in an alternative world, side by side with the happy people and yet somehow hopelessly removed from them.

Alfred looked heavenward and he felt so small and yet significant in the same breath. Something about him had always preferred the cold. The wind buffeted him, sweeping in from the fields and making him hunch his shoulders and turn the collar of his coat up as high as possible. He still had ground to cover before the road to the right, arrowing through thick woods which hid Hadamar from Berlin.

Today was Monday, which, Alfred now thought, was a good day, a day representing a whole week of opportunities. *To know, finally*, he daydreamed as he strode forward. The wind was whipping up and Alfred increasingly felt the cold, forcing him to hunch his shoulders higher and higher to defend himself, but there was little he could do against such elements. Like Party transmissions each evening, the chill insidiously crept under your skin. Alfred knew it would be hours before he was warm again.

He tucked his chin into his chest as another gust punished his face and he felt the rutted mud, caked by cold, crunching beneath the soles of his beaten school shoes. He knew his mother would be furious, he smiled in another new emotion he was discovering – gallows humour. Alfred looked up again out of the corner of his eyes. He was happy, but he knew the feeling was fleeting. For the first time in his life, Alfred was alone.

He crossed the empty road, heading out of the city, and gratefully ducked down the lonely track leading through the forest which was now a second home. Individual trees had become friends, swaying hello each afternoon and wishing him good fortune on his mission. They were his allies, shielding him from winds which discouraged him on his daily journey. They were helpless against the wall of wood and fir now harbouring Alfred.

It was not long before he had passed the end of the road, through the quiet path adjacent, and was approaching the wire announcing the perimeter of Hadamar hospital's grounds. *Keep out! Danger!* had concerned him on his first few visits, making him look nervously over his shoulder, like the eyes of Party spies were everywhere, poised to pounce, but Alfred had spent enough time here now to realise that the warnings were entirely empty. No one was coming.

Alfred reached forward and ran his fingers over the hard wire. Even this far from the hospital, Alfred could taste antiseptic on his tongue. He could not stand here today much longer. He was cold, he shivered. He walked along the wire fence, to the point where he was as close to the hospital as he could get. He held on to the wire and he dropped his head. He could not conceive a way through. The figures of hospital patients lived in the distance, visible to Alfred's naked eye and yet remaining unknowable from where he stood. He wanted to scream, wake up the world, but he did not hope anyone was listening.

Despite the icy chill, he pulled his hood off his head, so that he could see the patients walking about the hospital grounds in the distance. He noticed how their behaviour changed when briefly they were left alone. They blossomed for a moment, like a flower starved of sunlight, before their heads quickly bowed in submission as soon as anyone returned to police them once more.

Patients pushed awkwardly in old, wooden wheelchairs. Some walked aided by a frame. And some oddly ran freely, their impairment invisible to Alfred's eyes, watching through the wire and gripping it in frustration as he endlessly scanned the group from left to right, right to left for any sign of Meike. But nothing, never anything.

Alfred felt connected with Hadamar's patients in the short moments when they stood alone and laughed like teenagers, like normal, and as Alfred was discovering and beginning to think, only the Party had decided who was and was not 'normal' in Germany today.

A vehicle's rude roar then made Alfred jump and prick his finger on part of the wire. Blood pooled, he inspected up close, in the smallest circle. He sucked his finger and looked up and across at a bus arriving at the hospital entrance. He ran around to get a closer look. New patients, happy, excited. Two soldiers boarded the bus before shouts and a train of teenagers followed them off the vehicle, which had its windows blacked out. The teenagers chaotically grouped outside Hadamar's entrance before being herded in through the gaping front doors by the soldiers, struggling to keep control of the queue. Alfred could see that the children had a chance to dash for the safety of the woods right there and then. If they were quick like Alfred, he figured some would make it, but instead, the line of youngsters dutifully followed barked instructions and the back of the head of the person in front of them. Alfred then had an idea.

How could that work? It wouldn't. Too dangerous, his conscience debated. *Do you have a better idea?* the new devil in him then questioned.

38

With a start, Meike opened her eyes, sore from fractured sleep, to busy activity on her ward at Hadamar. Anxiety immediately dialled up in her body. It was late, she was late. People were busy making final preparations to receive the doctor, Devil No.1, on his morning rounds. *How? What?*

'Wakey, wakey, sleeping beauty,' Ingrid crooned to her left and Meike's instincts did not thank her for her sarcasm. *Where was the kind nurse?*

Meike wasted no time and quickly heaved herself up in bed before immediately flipping back rigid in spasm, her waist like a mechanical pivot. A coldness in Ingrid made her sit by and watch Meike struggle. Part of her wanted to help, but the doctor and nurses would be here any minute. It was Monday morning, *the* worst time to test them.

Meike successfully pulled herself up this time, stiffly, but it was a start and for a rare moment Meike wished her legs worked, just for a moment. Then, Ingrid smelt it first and she shot a harrowed look across to Meike, whose face quickly mirrored her panic. She was in trouble. *Oh no. Oh no.* A pungent heat flooded her senses from below. She knew it too well. It was never good. Meike had defecated herself in the night and now neither her father nor her grandmother were sympathetically on hand to help clean her and her soiled sheets quietly away, out of sight and out of mind. At times like this, she wanted to cry. She was a young woman.

She shifted in bed slightly to test the waters and she felt her bottom gruesomely squelch. From experience, she imagined excrement poured down the back of her thighs like sewage. There was not a lot to be done. She had no time, she had to get up, get to a bathroom and clean herself roughly off, and that was just to begin with. Meike knew she then faced the long process of emptying anything left remaining in her bowels before finally showering and cleaning herself so completely she smelt only of sunflowers in a spring meadow. Meike's heart would have sunk in her breast, but it was already full of dread.

In the bed opposite, a girl who did not speak spotted the discolouration of Meike's bed sheets, and she pointed and cowered, shrinking dramatically to the floor and drawing everyone's attention.

'Thanks,' Meike said under her breath, in an attempt at gallows humour, which right now was the least of her worries. *Where was the kind nurse?*

Progress. Meike had at least successfully shifted herself out of her seated squalor and now sat slightly more comfortably in her chair, which she had blanketed liberally with old sheets she was not permitted in Hadamar to keep spare for these emergencies. But the kind nurse had discreetly allowed it. The girl who did not speak opposite continued to point and cower. Meike wished she would stop. *Please stop.*

'Meike!' Ingrid whispered. Meike looked up and heeded the warning. He was here.

Devil No.1 strode into the space impatiently, wearing heavy bags under his eyes. Devil No.2 was close, face fixed sternly, like the very idea of Monday offended her. Meike craned her neck to her left, but there was still no sign of the kind nurse. The doctor was almost past Meike. He had no mood for real business today, merely to retreat to his office and a flask of schnapps out of sight in his desk drawer, normally reserved for Friday afternoons when he was too intoxicated by the prospect of drinking unhindered that evening to wait any longer. The odour from Meike's sheets ghosted up his nose and made him stop. He stood a yard past her bed. Hadamar's chief nurse was surprised, but then, too, smelt the warm stench rising from where Meike sat.

The doctor walked over to her slowly, a first smile of the day spreading on his lips. He loved authority. *His brothers weren't so perfect now, were they?* Rotting in some hellhole in some godforsaken corner of the eastern front. He would survive them both. What would his parents think then?

The hot odour of human stools beneath him brought his senses back to where he stood. He suddenly felt queasy, bile rising like lava up his throat. His face drained of colour like a sinkhole had opened up inside him, and his mouth was dry. He was dizzy. He was going to vomit. He was going to vomit.

The doctor took an unplanned pace forward towards Meike, sat perfectly still in her chair beneath him, but unable to escape her own smell. She was helpless. The doctor opened his mouth and bile jolted, retching from his throat and down Meike's face and breast, dripping into her lap. She squealed in discomfort. In the neighbouring bed, Ingrid scrunched her eyes shut to what was happening. Even Devil No.2 turned her face away, raising a hand to her mouth briefly.

The girl who did not speak pointed childishly at Meike before Devil No.2 paced over to the girl and slapped her across her face. Meanwhile, Devil No.1 turned again to face Meike and slowly began to unthread his leather belt from around his bulging waist. Unrestrained without it, his stomach spilled forward in folds.

'No!' Meike screamed, her pitch raking through the other patients' ears. Ingrid screwed her eyes tighter shut.

'Open your eyes, child!' Devil No.2 said loudly to Ingrid. 'Open your eyes... now!'

Ingrid opened her eyes to the glare of the chief nurse, stood across from her and motioning with her eyes to pay strict attention to the doctor and Meike. She submissively turned and pointed her chair in their direction like she had front row tickets at the theatre. She was just in time to catch the doctor carefully folding his belt in two, like he wished his own father had. Devil No.1 then threw his arm back in one, grand motion before bringing it down and striking Meike across her face and upper breast. He did not care where he struck. He was simply aiming for maximum damage.

Meike closed her eyes and she thought of and felt nothing as the strikes began to whip across her frame more and more. She strangely experienced their impact, but in the moment, she was spared their pain. The doctor began to tire, beads of sweat forming on his forehead like ants. He was handicapped by having to keep one arm clumsily at his waist, wrestling his trousers to remain up without a belt. He pulled back his arm once more in a short slingshot, heaving unhealthily, and he sliced Meike across her cheek, cutting her skin with a whip which made every other patient wince. It marked beneath Meike's eye, which quickly began to sting sharply.

Heartened by the strike, the doctor brought down his belt again now from on high, but he failed to connect at all as Meike flinched her head successfully out of the way. He was enraged. The doctor stepped forward into her smell and he grabbed her nightshirt by the shoulder, so that she could not move again.

'You... stupid... little... idiot...' he uttered, in time with four blows flowing down from his arm onto a helpless Meike. The doctor was now so spent physically that none of them had real force, but the intimacy of the assault made up for that and Meike wailed in distress, shielding her head with her hands as best she could. The lead nurse, Devil No.2, took a step forward.

Out of sight to the left, the ward's double doors bloomed open. A figure flashed in front of Ingrid before the sound of a thud followed by a smack on the ward's unforgiving floor and a skidding noise as the doctor skated on his back. Nobody could take back what they were witnessing.

Devil No.1 was afraid to clamber to his feet, instead peering up through his fear, but the kind nurse had already turned her back and was marching back away from him.

Devil No.2 was stunned and failed to make eye contact with her as she walked back past her, before she traced her gaze back to where Devil No.1 lay on the floor. She learnt something about him then. He had been cast out too.

The kind nurse was not waiting to hear what either of them had to say. She knew the consequences of her actions, pushing back open the double doors and exiting the ward, and then the hospital itself.

'Jew... idiot lover,' Devil No.2 whispered under her breath.

Outside, the kind nurse danced down the wide steps, leading up to Hadamar's entrance. In the heat of the moment, she had forgotten that the chief nurse knew precisely where she lived.

39

It was the following morning and Hadamar's chief nurse was pacing up flights of stairs in an apartment building in north Berlin. She was pursued by two officers from the Gestapo, struggling to keep up. The chief nurse felt her anger from yesterday rejuvenated, mixed now with an uneasy excitement. She was struggling not to smile and to let her teenage-like intoxication show. It felt thrilling to be on the frontline with the Gestapo. She could not remember feeling so alive. She intensified her purpose once more and forced the two officers behind her to breathe even more heavily, hiking up the spiral flights of stairs to the building's top floor, the cheapest rents.

The kind nurse, meanwhile, opened her eyes to a new day, a new start, which instinctively urged her to close them again to her changed circumstances following yesterday's dramatic events. Her conscience winced. What had she done? Happily, she had slept virtually straight through the night, her head puzzled. At least her thoughts were clear, she wondered, lying in bed and staring at the room's ceiling. She knew she couldn't return to Hadamar, her head told her. Part of her naturally wanted to get up and get ready for her shift, like it was normal, like it was any other day, but her mind reminded her it wasn't.

Hadamar's chief nurse was soon grateful she was climbing the final flight of stairs to the building's top floor apartments. Fatigue was starting to tighten her legs and she was increasingly holding on to a handrail running up each flight for support.

In bed, the kind nurse opened her eyes again. She had fallen back asleep and was uncertain for how long. Her eyelids felt less heavy. It was time to get up. She tipped her slender frame upright, bare feet kneading the floor beneath her like dough, as if she was preparing herself for what lay ahead, unchartered territory.

'Officers, the sixth floor. Apartment two,' the chief nurse said, having caught her breath to mutters of confirmation from the two men standing alongside her. She wanted badly to impress.

The kind nurse stood up and walked across the bedroom, out into the apartment's hallway en route to the bathroom, which was breathtakingly cold.

Hadamar's chief nurse wrung her hands as the two Gestapo officers she was accompanying gathered themselves and knocked loudly at the apartment door.

'State police!' they yelled above loud bangs on the door. 'Open up! Immediately.'

No answer. Only silence.

The kind nurse heard rude knocks at the door to the apartment, brushing her teeth in the bathroom. She was annoyed by the interruption and peered her head out into the hallway, dripping saliva from her mouth onto bare floorboards below.

The two officers banged again on the door, repeating their calls, while Hadamar's chief nurse watched behind them with rising impatience. Again, no answer. *Where is she?*

Are you going to get that? the kind nurse's head asked, picturing her flatmate, who she well knew was an early riser, long hearing telltale noises and voices in the apartment's kitchen.

More bangs at full volume from the two officers followed briefly by careful silence from the officers and chief nurse, listening intently for any signs of life. Nothing before the heavy sole of one of the men's boots kicked the door near the handle, breaking it off its hinges. It swung back and forth briefly.

The kind nurse froze, frowning at the noise. She finished cleaning her teeth and ventured back out into the hallway to see what all the fuss was. It was 8am, on the nose.

The two officers entered the apartment, impatient for sight of their target. Their eyes rifled through openings to rooms leading off the apartment's modest hallway. It seemed nobody was home. Finally, the men, with the chief nurse obeying orders and waiting outside, reached the last room on the corridor, what looked like a main bedroom, but it looked like it had not been slept in last night.

'Nurse!' an officer called and Hadamar's chief nurse anxiously paced inside, following the sound of her new colleague's voice. She had not slept well last night, instead replaying this moment in her mind, what she would say to the kind nurse. But in today's light, in vain.

'No one is here,' one of the officers told her flatly and she flushed with embarrassment, her mind immediately questioning, searching for an explanation. How could she have been wrong?

'She must be here,' the nurse called after herself, investigating each room in the small apartment herself. But nothing, no one.

'Check your information next time, Sister,' the officer said, making his way back out and leaving her alone in the apartment. 'Heil Hitler.'

'Yes,' the chief nurse said, casting her eyes down uncomfortably as the officers walked past. 'Heil Hitler,' she said, without conviction for once.

The kind nurse walked out of the bathroom, straight into her sister kissing another woman deeply.

'Edith... this is... Margot,' her sister said, wearing a smile only sex can elicit.

'Hi,' the kind nurse said awkwardly and still in her nightdress, which did a bad job of covering pretty knees.

'She has better legs than you,' Margot said, kissing and looking at the kind nurse's sister.

'Edith is just staying for a while... while she gets back on her feet,' her sister said, breaking off from the embrace. 'She's finally left that awful job I told you about at the old asylum from the Great War. They send spastics there now... freakshow.'

The kind nurse frowned. 'They're not freaks,' she said, before looking down once more uncomfortably at her toes. *Time to leave*, her conscience reminded her. It was time she visited Meike's grandmother.

40

'Heil Hitler, Mrs Richter,' said the kind nurse, stood at the bottom of the short steps leading up to her Berlin home.

'Heil Hitler,' Marta said neutrally, not failing to quietly examine the way her visitor had uttered the catch-all in Germany today. It had become almost code, how you declared it. The morning washed in brilliant sun, helping ease suspicions.

'I was a nurse at Hadamar, Mrs Richter.'

Marta's mind buckled under the weight of the words and everything they promised, threatened. Marta put out a hand and held a handrail close to their front door.

'I worked there until yesterday. I've been caring for your granddaughter, I believe, Mrs Richter – Meike. I would like to talk with you, if I may… inside, if that would be alright, so we can have some privacy.'

Marta's mind rushed with conclusions, too many and too quick for any attempt at clarity. Then, a thought jumped to the surface. *Meike was in Hadamar.* She had been right. She had been right, all of this time, despite people's protestations. They had been wrong, and she had been right. Then, her head sped up again with only questions.

How was Meike?
Was she alright?
How had she been? Has she been eating?
Is she able to maintain a routine in hospital?
Was she alright? Was she alright?

Marta dare not ask them for fear of learning the truth. All the time, the kind nurse waited patiently, standing politely on the Richters' front doorstep. Marta's hand on the supporting rail slipped and she started to fall, the kind nurse darting forward and catching her, and allowing her to lean on her like she had on duty a thousand times before.

'Mrs Richter, are you alright? I can only imagine how unsettling this must be,' she said, placing a trained hand behind the small of Marta's back. 'Why don't we go inside, sit down… I'll get you a glass of water… coffee, if you have some.'

'Yes… yes. Thank you… Miss?'

'It's Keller… Edith Keller,' she smiled, and, in that moment, Marta decided that she was genuine. She would listen to her.

The kind nurse helped Marta continue to straighten herself before the pair of them entered the house and closed the door on the world quietly behind them, making their way through the entrance hallway, in the shadow of the morning sun and entering Marta's square kitchen. Marta took a seat at the table and gathered herself for what she was about to hear. The kind nurse did not immediately take a seat, instead walking to the kitchen stove and taking the liberty of picking up a pot of coffee, now cold and holding it up to Marta, who nodded in reply. The kind nurse lit the stove and began reheating the pot before sitting down at the table opposite her.

Soon, the kind nurse was pouring coffee, wisping with heat, into two mugs, cloaking the air around them with its aroma. At the table, they sat together in silence for a moment and they each enjoyed a first sip. In her imagination, Marta nodded to herself. There was no more putting it off.

'Is... Meike okay?' she said, eyes closed and waiting.

'She is... she's quite well,' the kind nurse said, and Marta let out an enormous breath.

'Thank God,' she said, keeping her eyes closed as if she was guarding the moment for herself, and herself alone.

The kind nurse nodded slowly. She continued, 'She has been in Hadamar for the past six months. I remember her after she first arrived. I have always nursed on the ward where she has been. She's comfortable. It's not a bad place,' she said, lifting her coffee back to her lips to politely sip.

Marta exhaled again. She could feel her whole frame relaxing like a drug. Meike was safe. *She was safe*. And she had been cared for by the kind woman now sharing her kitchen table opposite her, but questions, Marta had so many questions.

'Why aren't we allowed to see her? Don't any parents go visit their children?' she asked.

The kind nurse hadn't been sure what questions to expect and yet, the kind nurse was troublingly appreciating that failing to answer any satisfactorily was in itself an answer, and one which revealed a truth she wanted to shield her host from.

'It is a difficult time... Mrs Richter,' the kind nurse began awkwardly, and Marta felt her hackles rise. 'We are at war...' the kind nurse said, still searching for the right words, but Marta was already shaking her head at her in disagreement.

'I know we're at war, Miss Keller,' she said tartly, and quickly regretted her tone.

A pause between them.

'It would be upsetting for everyone,' the kind nurse said, deciding to speak, 'if visitors were allowed at Hadamar. The Party has decided its course of action for someone in Meike's position and unfortunately, there is nothing you or I can do about it, at least for the time being.' The kind nurse hadn't meant to reach so far, and she feared Marta's response.

'If only I could see her,' Marta said like a confession, when the front door suddenly sounded behind them. A sound of normality. Hans, she presumed, lifting her eyes beyond her guest and looking down their hallway at where Hans stood, hanging his coat and scarf up. He met her eyes briefly and he nodded once. The kind nurse shuffled uncertainly where she sat.

'My husband,' Marta said, and the kind nurse nodded more happily, the pair of them waiting as Hans diplomatically went straight through to their front sitting room. They had privacy once more.

'Meike is surrounded by people her own age... and the nurses and doctors are very kind,' the kind nurse said with increasing unease. She wished she was better prepared, she thought, as she brought her cup up to her mouth like a shield against her disquiet, finishing the last of her coffee before they both stopped speaking for a moment as Hans poked his head into the kitchen where they sat.

'Good morning,' he greeted, and the kind nurse smiled politely back, but failed to reply, as if she needed her host's permission first. Marta, too, offered nothing, her eyes neutral, which Hans took as his cue to leave them both alone, which he did, returning to his newspaper in the sitting room. He wished his wife did not worry about Meike so.

Marta paused before picking the conversation back up. 'At Hadamar, Edith, did you know a boy called Horst?' she said, deciding to leave the question hanging while she collected their coffee cups from the table and walked them over to the kitchen sink.

'Yes,' the kind nurse said, suddenly stopping Marta in her tracks.

Marta turned back around to face her.

'I did, lovely boy... very gentle. Difficult... with his condition,' she said before her curiosity interrupted her. 'Why?'

'How did he die?' Marta said, choosing to turn her back again on her guest. She paused her task in the sink awaiting a response.

'Horst... didn't die, Mrs Richter,' the kind nurse said, choosing to return to formality. 'I think if the doctors at Hadamar were being honest, they would have said his needs were too great for them. He returned home to his parents.'

Marta turned around and her emotion was momentarily softened by sunlight dancing on the kitchen table. From her seat, the kind nurse briefly studied Marta's age and the toll her granddaughter's absence had perhaps taken, white hairs invading her temples like the tide before diverting her focus for fear of insulting her. Marta lowered herself back into her seat at the table.

'Horst is dead, Miss Keller,' Marta said, timing her words and not making eye contact. 'He died at Hadamar. I must know if Meike, too, is in danger, Miss Keller,' she said. 'In real danger... I would never forgive myself.' Marta reached across the divide between them, taking hold of one of the kind nurse's hands. But the nurse did not appreciate the touch and she gently released her hand from Marta's.

The kind nurse's conscience tugged at her like a child pleading with a parent to read one more story before bedtime.

'How do you know Horst is dead, Mrs Richter?' she said and there was uneasy eye contact between the two of them.

'I met with his mother,' said Marta. 'She received a letter from Hadamar informing them that Horst had died from pneumonia. They had cremated his body immediately on safety grounds,' she recounted. Marta felt momentarily as if Horst's mother was sat beside them at the kitchen table. 'She could have her son's ashes mailed, if she wished, at no expense.'

The kind nurse processed the rush of detail. Her instincts were both trusting and disbelieving all at once.

'Horst could have been transferred to another hospital, Mrs Richter,' the kind nurse said, but she was almost doubtful herself.

'He could have been… you're right,' said Marta, who noticed the kind nurse pulling at a ring on her engagement finger, the first time her body language had betrayed her. 'Do you have someone fighting on the front?' Marta asked and the kind nurse laughed a little, which felt like both a relief and a warning.

'No,' the nurse said. 'I don't… the army would be the last place for him.'

Marta nodded.

'Meike was attacked by a doctor yesterday,' the kind nurse suddenly said breathlessly. 'She had had an accident… in bed in the night. It wasn't her fault… How could we? We're supposed to care for our patients… aren't we?'

Marta looked at the nurse gravely, and the entire mood in the kitchen seemed to change.

'I could not stand by,' the nurse said, almost in reassurance. 'I haven't gone to work today. I fear I may be arrested.'

Silence for what felt like a long time and then eye contact, meaningful eye contact between the two of them.

'Thank you,' Marta mouthed, trying her best to contain her rising panic. 'Thank you.'

41

Meike opened her eyes in darkness and awoke with an unsettling disorientation. Where was her chair? Where was she?

She was outside in an icy death, black and silent like whales. She felt a horribly long way from home and vulnerable, like mother nature could swallow her whole at any moment. A shady figure swam into Meike's view, hunched upright, neighbouring Meike and yet somehow removed on the freezing ground. The figure was traced by an outline as the darkness began to forgive and Meike's heart quickened, pulsing heat through her chest. The figure sat silent and obedient, but obeying who?

Meike's senses were sharpening more and more in the deep, which became clearer to her, more known. The two of them were sitting outside on grass. Meike's companion was a girl chattering uncontrollably, like the cold had taken control of her and she was now helpless to its grip. Watching her, sat cross legged nearby, Meike was only reminded how cold she was herself, how it was sunken in her chest like an anchor. Meike knew from experience how much effort it took to reach down and pull it out.

42

Marta heard the front door to their home click close, the kind nurse pulling it quietly shut behind her. The sound seemed to turn off a switch inside her that she had been unable to reach until now. She stood upright and leant her head back so that her eyes cast up to the ceiling in their kitchen, though she was unable to focus. She reached down and she placed a hand on their wooden table to steady herself as she climbed to her feet, lighter, rushing with the headiness of the information she had just received.

'Is everything alright?' Hans said, walking up the hallway to their kitchen and tilting his head to one side, as though an invisible pillar separated them.

'She's there,' Marta said, head bowed and eyes unable to meet her husband's. 'She's there, Hans.'

'Who's where, darling?' he said, confused.

Marta's mind scoffed ill-temperedly at the question. He hadn't believed her from the start, the devil on her shoulder pointed out, the recollection jabbing at her conscious. In her mind, Hans had always been playing catch-up. She turned and she began filling their sink with water and a thin foam only, helping save on soap, to wash this morning's breakfast dishes. Hans watched his wife from where he remained standing. He knew what she was doing.

Marta turned back to him to find his face searching hers. She hated hating her husband and yet now her instincts allowed precious competing feelings to creep into her heart, even for Hans, especially for Hans. She felt consumed by a thirst to find their youngest granddaughter.

'*She* is there, Hans,' she said. 'That place... in *that* hospital... *we* visited. And they turned us away... told *us* to go home.'

'You know for certain Meike's at Hadamar? For certain?' he said, almost like an accusation.

Marta tried not to scream and instead placed both her hands on their supper table to try and somehow allow the anger to drain from her. She turned away from him and faced the window looking out to their back garden.

'This is Meike... Meike, Hans!' she said, her hands locked on to the kitchen sink's edge. 'She's there, Hans... she is there! The woman just here is a nurse who has cared for her these past few months. She's seen her every day... every day,' said Marta, repeating herself like she was also convincing her own subconscious. 'And she didn't know, Hans, that Horst, Mrs Kohler's boy, was dead. She didn't know. What does that say? What does that say? They are hiding something, Hans, at that hospital. I know it... we must go and get her,' she said, but her anger was fading fast. She wished Hans would rush across their kitchen to catch her.

Hans remained stood opposite her, eyes fixed down slightly. He walked quietly past her to their kitchen sink and began washing his glass and plate from this morning. Marta was filled with frustration once more.

'Oh, leave that!' she spat, roughly reaching around him and turning off the tap. 'Are you going to help me, Hans? Help find her? I need you, Hans. Meike needs you... she needs us.'

Hans stood still, turned awkwardly but not fully away from Marta. He looked out from their kitchen window, at their suburban back garden and unruly green hedge tops, reaching eight, maybe nine, feet tall. They badly needed cutting back and yet this year Marta had failed to berate him for not doing so. Behind him, she watched him eyeing them.

Hans found his imagination looking through their back garden and vividly picturing a tiny Meike, a ball of blonde, scampering around and giggling at his feet. If anyone had walked into their home and threatened a hair on her head, he would have knocked them stone cold out, or worse, in another life. But not this one. This was all there was. Hans's memory stopped playing the scene, like an old film reaching the end of the reel. He turned around to face his wife and looked at her uncertainly. He had secretly feared for years that he had left all the fight he had in him in France, in 1918, before returning home that November forever defeated.

Marta's eyes pierced her husband's, imploring him for a response, any response, but nothing, which was all she needed to hear before reaching for and wrapping a scarf around her neck. She pulled her coat on and turned her back on her husband. She walked down their hallway to their front door. She paused before opening it and walking out into the world.

43

Meike was unsettled by the hoot of an owl, close and haunting, before the swishing of wings away from where they sat signalled its departure into the black. Meike tried again to tuck herself up as tightly as her disobedient legs would allow, sat on glacial grass. She could feel the cold creeping into her bones, like it was able to reach up from the ground and slowly wind around her like a vine. She was wearing only a nightgown, which felt thinner than cigarette paper.

Neighbouring her, the apparition of a girl continued to shake without making a sound. Meike began to recognise parts of her, a young woman, older, eighteen perhaps, but in Meike's mind more closely resembling a teenage boy, growth checked by a diet of trauma. Meike couldn't recall her name, which frustrated her, but in a way that was welcome. Exasperation was the first familiar thing she had experienced since waking up in this place. Meike let out a gasp of ice and puffed out two hard breaths to try and somehow galvanise her chest into action and warmth.

'Is it... Margarete?' Meike spoke in first words between them, which sounded like a shock.

The girl's head turned immediately, like the owl above them, before a firm shake no. *Oh... what was it?* Meike yearned to remember and more alert, she was reminded to unwind her body to check her bare legs, which seemed now to be stapled with goose bumps and turning a disturbing blue. Meike breathed hard again, and white clouds puffed out of her mouth, lingering for a moment, before the black swallowed them.

Meike nodded to herself, and she was heartened by the realisation of the familiar, which defused part of her fear. This was the field where patients at Hadamar were allowed out each afternoon, unaccompanied even for blissfully rare moments. But, in the distance, the wall of wire surrounding them was always watching, sentient like, separating them from the outside world and any hope that they remained a part of it. Beyond the wire, the treeline stood benign and untouched like the ocean, reassuringly beyond the hospital's control.

Meike knew where she was now, but why? And with only their nightshirts on? Why had they been singled out? Meike propped herself up, using one hand and an arm as a pillow, and she began dragging her legs like anchors into herself before slowly sliding across to her neighbour, who remained tightly huddled.

The girl looked at Meike blankly through waves of shivers before unfolding her frame like an angel and pulling Meike and her stone legs into a more comfortable position next to her. The touch of each other's skin was startling at first, their thin bodies kissing like uncertain lovers. The owl was back and close, hooting once more, less haunting now and reassuring, perhaps, that it, after all, was a friend.

Meike huddled into the girl's flat breast, burrowing into her like wild siblings. The shock of each other's skin was thawing and slowly warming, their shivers taking voice once more and jarring like the world was shaking in miniature. Meike could hear them both chattering and was comforted, the smallest smile beginning to trace across blue lips. She dared to turn her eyes outward, casting their gaze to the tops of trees in the distance. The thinnest glow was drawing over them. It was dawn, dawn was breaking.

44

Meike and the girl who looked like a teenage boy huddled in bed back on the ward in the relative warmth. They each lay under painfully thin bed sheets, like pieces of ice stubbornly refusing to thaw. Out of the two of them, Meike was shaking the worst, her teeth chattering together like castanets. Her legs, paralysed by poor circulation, could not get warm, while above her waist, her frame shuddered. What had they done to deserve this?

She pulled what covering she could over herself once more and winced. She felt like last night's induced insomnia had given her two black eyes. She tugged the one pillow she had tighter, underneath her leaden head for any comfort she could muster.

She purposely closed her eyes where she lay, curled in bed, and tried to transport herself to some place, any place else. She felt like last night had left a bruise on every bone in her body. She thought of Alfred, which surprised her. She had once exclusively liked 'bad' boys, who were almost always older. Now, lying here, she only wanted to be loved.

When was the last time I ate? she thought. How many days had it been since she had been moved to this new ward? She saw now that she had it good, back on her old ward in her bed neighbouring Ingrid, where the kind nurse could watch out for her, help her. Since the day the doctor assaulted her, she sported a cut underneath one eye, making her look like someone who courted trouble. If she changed her expression without thinking, the slice on the top of her cheek nipped her face like an invisible crab.

Alfred's face flashed again in her imagination. She recalled his laugh fondly and how it instinctively made her smile in reply. The small must of his smell, still polite in its odour after exercise. He was a boy, after all. She smiled. Her cheek!

Meike opened her eyes again, balled up tightly in bed. She was beginning to graduate to somewhere between cold and okay, but that was only her temperature, not this place or this ward she had been moved to away from Ingrid and the rest on what looked like, now lifting her head with an effort, a ward of waking dead. A patient, a boy, crouched down not far from Meike's bed. He was shirtless and dirty, and he smelt, Meike thought, peering at him as he began licking a mop. Meike could not fathom why until she recognised that he was sucking moisture from the end of its tips. *What is this place?* Meike's heart sobbed.

In his chest, Alfred could feel his heart today ache for Meike. A car loudly busied by him, heading back into the city with two National Socialist flags fluttering on the front. Alfred half turned around to watch its black rear sailing away from where he stood on the roadside, heading out into rural Germany. The sight of the two flags made his heart hurt, when they flew past. He knew worst was to come later tonight following supper: the Party's evening wireless broadcast, poisoned thoughts seeping insidiously like gas into the consciousness of every family in Berlin.

In the last few days, Alfred had studied in the dictionary the meaning of 'conspiracy' more than once, in an effort to understand it better, pinpoint its precise meaning, but it hadn't helped. Alfred could not fathom Party arguments and yet, by the end of each broadcast, which seemed to his teenage ears to grow increasingly frantic in its claims, Alfred always found his conscience siding with Mr and Mrs Huber, who ran their local fruit and vegetable shop. At least lately, Alfred had not had to worry about queuing to get the items on his mother's list he always placed tightly in his pocket. He turned his attention back to the here and now, and where he was, and he was angry with himself for almost missing the turn off the main road leading down the wooded track to Hadamar. *Eight, nine. Nearly there.*

Each day, Meike could feel herself weakening, a lethargy creeping up her like the tide. She feared she was beginning to struggle to keep her head above water. Each morning when she woke, her head thumped like the Christmas Day she drank too much of her grandfather's schnapps, which, of course, Anselma had not been guilty of, her sister's eyes fixing on her the following day like she was a medical experiment to only be learnt from, not engaged with. The accompanying hunger pangs and now pregnant swelling in Meike's belly were worse first thing, instantly reminding her that she had failed to eat the evening before. How much longer could she live like this?

When the pain within her belly was worse, Meike lurched forward where she sat, desperately holding her stomach together like she might otherwise fall apart. She was quickly learning why her fellow patients hardly spoke here on this ward. Simple survival was privately taking them prisoner.

Meike chose to turn her frame over in bed, as gingerly as she could, as if she was made of glass. Her body ached with cold like it had become part of her.

Ten, Alfred repeated in his head for confirmation. Then chaos. Alfred looked up, shaking his head briefly to free himself from the memory. He was surrounded by rich trees shielding Hadamar from the road and passing eyes travelling into Berlin. He felt calm beneath their towering reach. It was the only moment in his days now when his head stopped spinning, blissfully briefly, walking among these mighty guardians. He could simply be.

Meike had to go to the bathroom. She really didn't want to, and she couldn't conceive moving from her current position, coiled tightly in bed to protect what little warmth she had been able to generate over the previous few hours, or had it been days? Here, who could tell with any real confidence? She saw a blur of her button nose, peeking out from the white pillow which cushioned the side of her face. It looked pink and fleshy again after she had spent half of the previous night watching her skin turn an alien blue.

The older girl who looked like a boy made her heart jump, surprising her and appearing at her bedside, stepping softly in bare feet, which had lost their gender through dirt and wear. The girl leant forward, whispering so peacefully in her ear that Meike could barely recognise words, simply a feeling.

'Would you like to transfer to your chair?' she hushed, while her eyes looked beyond the two of them.

Meike nodded, before quickly feeling her face start to tremble with tears, not because she was upset, but because someone was showing – no, reminding – her that they cared.

Alfred walked up to Hadamar's wire perimeter, which had become something of an old friend these last weeks and months, not someone he could honestly say he liked, but at least understood. That said something. Alfred reached out to experience its touch, like a heavy drinker pondering a first glass of the evening, allowing the temptation to linger momentarily before hastily swallowing its contents. He was here. Once again, he had made it this far and hope surged through him, warming his frame. Today might actually be the day.

He lifted his head slowly to survey the expanse of flat ground before him, plain and unkempt for 150 metres, he had approximated, until his eyes first witnessed the gentle gathering of the hospital's patients grouped outside at this time of the afternoon. He continued to lift his eyes slowly, not daring to raise them too quickly, which he had on some days and then had instantly regretted when there was no sign of Meike, as if God was punishing his impatience. *Wait, Alfred. Wait. Ten,* he repeated in his head for confirmation.

Meike sat in her chair with the girl who looked like a boy standing over her.

'Shall we go outside?' the girl whispered in her ear.

Yes, Meike nodded, determined to face the outside again so soon after their ordeal. She fixed a look on her face that said it refused to be afraid.

The girl pushed her to the door leading out into Hadamar's grounds and Meike was paying her a real compliment, because, if she could help it, Meike did not permit anyone to push her unaided in her chair, which had grown in the time since to become part of her following her accident. Its once cold contours had softened until loved ones could see only human shapes and curves, metal or skin, when they tried to hide the sadness locked in their eyes when they looked at her. They were one and the same now.

The front edge of Meike's chair framing her feet stuck out, making it useful, though, Meike had decided, not by design for bumping open doors, which now transported her exposed into an immediately unforgiving wind, blowing across the hospital grounds, wide open to the elements. The sky domed overhead was grey, unfeeling.

Meike braved the chill, scrunching her face up as if it was possible to hide it somehow from the gale, squinting through its buffeting bid to persuade her back inside, where it was warm and safe from its howls. The girl pushed Meike out into the grounds where they had been only twelve hours previous and yet, as they looked about the landscape, it was disturbing how difficult it was to recognise precisely where they had been.

'Are you okay?' the girl hushed, leaning over Meike, who nodded.

'I'm okay,' she said, turning around to look at her companion. Then, the smallest miracle as the sun peered out, washing the area in sunlight like fresh sheets falling over a newly made bed; luxury. Meike sat in her chair and tilted her face skyward almost imperceptibly. She closed her eyes to soak up the sun's reach. Everything felt less sore suddenly before shadows closed across Meike's eyelids and she opened them only to overwhelming grey once more. But not entirely, the sun had reminded her that it had not yet abandoned this place.

'Let's go back inside,' the girl who looked like a boy mouthed, and Meike was surprised at how quickly she was able to learn how to lipread her new friend. Meike peered in the distance and noticed a figure on the horizon, the wrong side of the wire, the side where Berlin ended and Hadamar and its cruelty began. The girl who looked like a boy stood still in bare feet, muddy underneath. She noticed Meike's focus was diverted and cast her gaze in the same direction, across the flat no man's land no patient had crossed.

Meike began to open her mouth before the girl shook her head and pursed her lips in reply. She knew what she was going to ask. Meike wished she could make the individual out more clearly, but they stood too distant to decipher. The wire obscured their frame, and they were wearing a hood turned up against the chill. The figure looked back at her through time.

It couldn't be. Alfred stood 150 metres away, gripping the wire fence like his hands were glued to it. He pulled back his hood so his view was as uninhibited as possible.

It was her.

It was her!

Was it her? Alfred's mind was rushing with so much adrenaline he could not think. It was her. It was her. It was

Meike, he was certain. It was her. He had found her. *He had found her.*

Alfred watched her turn and be pushed in her chair by another patient, a boy it looked like, which stupidly riled his teenage jealousy and threatened to spoil the moment, but that didn't matter now. He watched the pair of them push through a door leading back into the main building. He recognised the back of Meike's head, her hair, her soft shoulders. She had been here this whole time, each time and afternoon he had dutifully visited, hidden somewhere behind Hadamar's walls. She appeared thin to him, from what he remembered of her pretty face, which had sparkled like magic up close. Alfred stayed as long as he could after she disappeared back inside the hospital before deciding to head back home. With the wind at his back and his thighs surging like a thoroughbred, Alfred flew.

45

Sunlight lit the Berlin morning up. *It is a good omen,* thought Father Maier, Marta's local priest, looking up at the perfect sea of blue above before pacing inside church and trying to ignore the sense of portent brewing in his belly. He began politely placing Bibles out for parishioners along church pews ahead of today's service, a task more usually reserved for a less senior colleague, but today Father Maier had insisted. He took a breath and clasped a final Bible to his chest like he was giving up his personal copy, not daring to lift his eyes too high, up to the church's towering ceiling, as had become his wont over the years he had served in this quarter of Berlin. Was he doing right? The danger of what he was intending to commit to record had troubled his sleep all week.

He let go of the Bible within his grasp and placed it carefully down like a mother might rest her baby's head at night, his fingers feathering the worn front cover tenderly. He had to speak out, he reminded himself, resolving once more. There was no more hiding in the everyday, not now. It was not right. *He* was right. '*Have faith,*' he whispered to himself, recalling his mentor's mantra before he was adorned fresh from studying theology at university.

Those two words were soon drowned out by the thump of his heart in his chest, stood in his pulpit, looking out over an expectant congregation, waiting to receive his weekly message. *Why did each pew have to be so packed today?* he thought selfishly, looking down at his notes one final time. *Have faith*, his mind tried once more.

Father Maier's eyes surveyed the congregation as if he was fly fishing on his day off. Soldiers in uniform. Men in SS uniforms. Wives and sweethearts. Sons handsome and pretty daughters. Widows. And Mrs Schulze, who he had to have particular patience for. And, lastly, in the front rows, Marta and Hans, with Anselma, their now lone granddaughter still at home. No Meike. No Abbe, he then remembered, and close by, Horst's mother and a space next to her, untaken. *Have faith*, he told himself again. He began speaking.

His sermon had opened innocently enough, Marta thought, sat tight in her seat in church. She gripped her husband's hand in anticipation, which made him turn his head to her and smile as best he could. He admired her so, though he wished he could find a way to finally tell her. He was glad Meike had her grandmother fighting for her.

Marta continued to fix her look steadfastly forward, he noticed, though the smallest flick of her eyes told him that she was aware of everything, terror almost locking her head in position.

'We are privileged,' Father Maier said, referring to his notes like a safety blanket, though he always knew by heart the words he would use each Sunday. 'Privileged to be witness to a great time.'

The National Socialists among the congregation looked at the uniformed men among them and exchanged eyes in reverence to their company.

'And privileged to bear witness to a moral catastrophe right before us.'

Eyes become less certain.

'The future is watching us, and how we react and respond. How do you wish to remember what is happening today through parts of Germany and in our corner of our country's capital?'

A husband and his wife shared a raised eyebrow and whisper. It was unlike the church to talk openly about the Jewish problem. They shrugged in casual acquiescence.

'There is a quiet genocide being committed in Berlin today,' Father Maier continued. 'Perhaps discreetly by our neighbours, but tacitly by every one of us… if we bear witness and yet choose not to intervene.'

Father Maier turned a page in his notes, the rustle of paper eerily audible among everyone sat silent. In the front rows, Marta continued to stare forward, trapped in her silence. This, she thought, was the soliloquy she had asked him to deliver. She squeezed her husband's hand tightly.

'There is an effort currently underway in Berlin to erase a class of human beings… to eliminate them from society, but which will only have a final purpose of impoverishing our lives and our legacy,' Father Maier said, leaving most parishioners now staring wide eyed at one another. 'We must act now,' he said. 'In moral defiance of that effort, in a way we would wish ourselves if we were to sit down with God and be judged.'

He looked up from his notes and his eyes faltered for

the first time when he witnessed, from the church pews, the stares arrowing back at him.

More secret whispers now between the mouths of spouses being shared like kisses and making Father Maier pause. For Marta, stationed in the front row with what felt like an ocean of water building behind her, the weight was unbearable. *This is your fault*, the air behind her hissed.

Agitated shuffles swelled in waves and were deafening in their discomfort. Marta gripped Hans's hand again and turned her head towards him, the relief of movement palpable, making him hold her eyes in his tenderly and attempt to pour all his love into a single look.

A loud cough from the back of church made Marta sit back forward. Like a distant firefight in battle, trouble was coming whether they liked it or not. In every bone, Marta felt she could bear it no longer, flushing from her head to her toes with red guilt. Anselma sat beside them still blankly and wondered plainly why Father Maier didn't simply say the word 'Jew' and be done with the dilly-dallying. She looked impatiently behind her, and she wished the service was over already so that she could gossip with her friends from the LGG.

'National Socialism is inviting us to board a train,' Father Maier said, with audible unease now pervading every pew.

Marta's heart was thumping so loudly in her breast it was beginning to hurt. She braced herself before the sight of Horst's mother sat alone at the end of a pew opposite distracted her. Horst's mother's grief had marked her out as a pariah as plainly as any yellow star. Marta wished she had the courage to go and sit beside her.

From his pulpit, Father Maier continued to speak, catching the eye of senior army officers, invincible in their uniform and all it represented. He closed his eyes to their sight and yet, like Marta, he could not help but feel their burning disapproval reflecting back at him. *Have faith*, he reminded himself.

'Where is this train heading?' he questioned, raising his head as he did so. 'But those of us who care to ask earnestly will disembark in favour of what they believe to be right... what they believe, regardless of the consequences. It is a warning,' Father Maier said, beginning to regain confidence. 'A warning... to each of us, and a dilemma: how would we wish to be treated were our own circumstances less fortunate?'

But only murmurs and uncomfortable coughs from the congregation grew again.

'Handicapped people, young and old, share the same dreams, the same desires as all of us... to live life fully, work, be productive... contribute. Love. Be happy... grow old... have children.'

'Rubbish!' a voice cried out from the back of the church, making whole rows of people turn around noisily in unison. The yell made Marta jump in her seat. Her entire being was on alert. More noise now, communal. The sound of people climbing to their feet and leaving. An immutable message all of its own.

Marta continued to grip Hans's hand. She instinctively glanced across to Mrs Kohler, at the front of the church, but she was only looking forward. Above them, the priest glanced down at his sermon notes, only in pause before increasing the volume of his voice. *Have faith*.

He spoke, 'If we fail to act now in defiance of this genocide at Hadamar hospital…'

His words were met by a gasp from one woman followed by Mrs Jaeger, of the Women's League, climbing from her seat, wearing a look of disgust as Anselma shot an ashamed look over her shoulder at the emptying church.

'Come, child… away from this nonsense,' Mrs Jaeger called to Anselma, rising too from her seat and drawing a gasp from Marta.

'Leave her,' Hans whispered into her, holding tight to her hand. Marta relented and thought she was going to cry.

Multiple people were now rising from their seats, diluting the power of Father Maier's service, which was drowning in the commotion. No one wearing a uniform remained.

Father Maier raised his head and he saw only islands of people, not a throng, isolated and separate.

'If we fail to act,' Father Maier said more gently, given the intimacy of his remaining audience, 'who will be next in line to be taken from our streets, our homes? It is the moral call of our day to stand against – demand – the release of patients from Hadamar. Who will join me next Sunday?' he asked, raising his head confidently, smiling and nodding quietly to some. 'Will you march with me on Hadamar, where we will stand and will remain until the authorities answer our call and decide to release our children back into our homes and communities? Will you join me?' he said once more, eyes drawn to Marta.

'Thank you,' she mouthed.

46

Meike woke and was quickly reminded where she was. Then, the smell hit her first. *Oh no. Oh no!* Faeces, she could smell faeces. It was a nightmare start to the day.

She ripped off bed sheets and expected to discover that she had defecated herself while sleeping, but she couldn't see anything, which raised her spirits briefly. The whipped sound of sheets, blooming out beneath her and unveiling white skin on her young legs, puffed with paralysis, was the first sound she had recognised in days. Its familiarity felt galvanising before the injection of morale was instantly dulled by what felt like a needle embedded in her head. Dehydration. She needed to drink. Water. And lots of it, to cure this constant hangover weighing her down like an anchor.

One of her legs jangled loose, slipping off the side of the bed like butter before she realised that she had not made a mess in her sleep. Thank the Lord. *Thank the Lord!* She felt a rush of relief. She was clean, well, as clean as she could be now that she was without the kind nurse's, or any nurse's, daily visits to help manage her routine. Meike searched beneath one of her soft thighs to explore what she quietly feared. Bed sores, worsening, like invasions of red exploding in miniature on her skin. Tilting herself in bed as best she could, so she could widen her view, she winced. She couldn't afford for them to become worse. Sores became infected, Meike's memory parroted, mimicking her doctor's unfeeling advice in the days following her accident, and infections, left untreated, would slowly leach into her blood, poisoning her. Meike tried not to shudder, allowing the bottom of her thighs to fall back out of sight. *Out of mind, for now*, Meike thought, lifting her head and blinking like each motion reset a button in her brain, even only a little. This fog which had been clouding it.

Meike, balanced upright in bed, turned her head to her right and noticed something out of reach on her bedside cabinet, something different. A jug of water, a full jug of water waiting invitingly alongside an empty glass. That had not been there before as she woke in the morning. Adrenaline trickled through her frame. Water. Meike wasn't waiting on ceremony. With both hands flat by her hips, she began pushing herself, inch by deliberate inch, closer to the side of the bed, where she could transfer into her chair and then – then – begin greedily quenching her thirst.

Meike jumped down to her chair roughly, more roughly than she would have normally allowed, but what else was she to do? She felt an instinct of something in her calf, which the same unfeeling doctor assured her was really not possible and yet Meike knew what her body was telling her. She looked down and saw that it was telling her that she had cut her leg. It didn't look too bad, she shrugged, thoughts overtaken by her thirst.

She hitched herself into a more comfortable position before turning clockwise to face the jug of water, pristine and poised. Her mind was consumed by the thought of it running down her throat like a stream and watering her insides, which felt like dust. *This headache. Not for much longer*, she told herself, reaching out a hand.

Meike picked up the jug from the bedside cabinet, laden with water and she immediately almost dropped it through weakness in her grip. She had misjudged how heavy it was. *Careful, Meike*, she told herself before clumsily sloshing water into a glass quickly filled with its precious contents. She lifted it to her lips, savouring the anticipation briefly. She was going to feel better. She was going to be better.

Meike tilted the glass to her lips. *Bang.*

Jarring. Jumping. Meike cried out and she felt a throb on her lips where the glass had thumped against them before splintering to the floor. Her heart and her head pounded, and she turned to her left to see the rest of the ward and a waft of faeces crept up her nose again, before the tall girl who looked like a teenage boy swam into her view. She leant into Meike, who was too dumbstruck to recoil.

'Salt water... don't drink. It's a trick,' she hushed, pulling her eyes away at an odd angle. Meike moved the tops of her fingers up to her face to discover if her lip was bleeding. Nothing. She then tasted drops of moisture left on her lips. Salt, unmistakably. The girl was right.

'Quick, quick... idiots! Idioooots,' voices crooned in an echo, carrying louder and louder towards them. The girl who looked like a boy spurred into action, surprising Meike, and immediately threw the water out of the jug, splashing it across the wall behind them. She hurried behind Meike and sat perfectly still, only following her companion with her eyes.

'We have to go… quickly,' she hushed.

'Okay,' said Meike and the girl immediately began pushing her as the ward's double doors behind them now thumped open, revealing two soldiers, hardly older than boys, holding a large hose. They started to spray patients as they came across them.

'Time for morning showers! Useless eaters!'

'Useless shitters!' the second soldier mimicked, sporting a gas mask, and his colleague laughed as they hosed a boy down where he lay in bed in excrement. The spray was obscene. The girl pushed Meike in her chair faster and faster towards the doors at the opposite end of the ward.

'Hey… hey!' one of the soldiers shouted at them, but neither Meike nor the girl looked back, surging only forwards and focused on the prize within their reach. *Smack*. A sharp thud and a deep wince. Meike turned her head and the girl who looked like a boy laid splayed on the floor sodden with water from the hose which had now knocked her off her skeletal feet.

'Got you!' a voice shouted behind them.

The soldier ran towards them and slipped in his haste on thin faeces swimming on the floor. His stumble urged the girl back to her feet, back behind Meike, thrusting her forward in her chair once more as Meike gripped the arms of her chair for dear life, fearing she may be tipped dangerously forward and spill out herself. Any injury could be fatal. Meike's leg bones, not used to the weight of her body, were now only made of glass.

The girl who looked like a boy picked up her pace and she began dashing the final few metres to the ward's double doors, leading out into a corridor.

'Stop... stop!' one of the soldiers cried, slipping and sliding the whole time like he was skating on the ward's flooded floor. Part of Meike wanted to obey the order, but there was no time and she braced herself for the bang through the doors, scrunching her eyes shut almost. *Bang*.

The doors flushed open, smacking the corridor walls as they continued to fiercely push forward. Meike opened her eyes. They were through. They had made it.

'Here,' the girl hushed with a breathless pant now in Meike's ear, and the pair of them hurriedly wheeled, more carefully this time, into a cramped toilet on the corridor. The girl meticulously locked the door behind them to the sound of the same double doors banging open once more. Brief silence followed by pants of young, male breath.

'Out... out, idiots! Come out now,' a soldier crooned again. Then, loud thumping in turn on each door up and down the corridor, making Meike jump each time as the noise neared them. Meike and the girl huddled at the back of the unnervingly small room.

Bang.

Bang.

Bang. The soldiers had reached their door.

Each thunder of noise was like an alarm in Meike's heart, jumping in response in panic. Scared, she looked up to the girl who looked like a boy. *Should we give ourselves up?* Meike's eyes said. The girl slowly shook her head *no* like a pendulum and its motion helped slow Meike's booming heart. The girl placed her palm in the centre of Meike's breast to help her breathing. The pair of them shared a smile thin with fear, but it was the beginning of something greater in both of them. A refusal.

'Out! Out, idiots… now,' a soldier yelled. The crooning was gone now and Meike's panic rose up her throat once more. The girl who looked like a boy whispered in a perfect hush, which Meike could only make out in the softest patter of syllables, ephemeral, like her breath on an icy night.

'I didn't hear you,' Meike said before realising her mistake. Too loud. She was too loud, trying once more and placing a single hand on one of the girl's arms as if it would help her communicate. 'I couldn't hear you,' she mouthed. A pause and a moment between their eyes.

'We don't have to do anything,' the girl whispered.

47

'Good morning, Father Maier,' greeted Marta outside her local church. It was Sunday, and her and Hans were the first to arrive. They were the only ones to arrive so far.

'Good morning, Marta... Hans,' Father Maier said, glad to see someone at least. His face was written with anxiety, which he always felt was intrinsic to his duty to hide. Priests, after all, had to calm people from the unfathomable, but this morning he was failing to, and Marta and Hans noticed, sharing a worried glance. Father Maier looked up to the heavens before quickly admonishing his vanity, or worse, his selfishness. What made him special? *Have faith*, he said in his head.

The three of them stood in the Berlin street, outside the church entrance. They each felt the oddness of that. It was a Sunday. At this time, they should be *inside* church. Marta and Hans tried unconvincingly to make small talk between the three of them, but it was distracted. Their group felt achingly small. Father Maier's eyes wandered before catching sight of the ubiquitous National Socialist flags festooning sides of buildings up all along the street they stood on. Each time one of the flags flapped in the morning wind, Father Maier thought its portent was personal, a code only he could decipher, and yet he had no earthly idea if its translation was malignant or benign. Which did he fear most?

'Heil Hitler,' a passing couple out walking greeted, the man raising his hat slightly, while the woman seemed to smile only sadly.

'Heil Hitler,' Father Maier and Marta said, more assured. Hans offered nothing, drawing daggers from Marta's face before a disarming shrug soon made her smile. Father Maier remained restless where he stood, almost pacing on the spot. Where were other members of his congregation, ready to join and support their march on Hadamar hospital?

A crow cawed overhead, underlining the unease the three of them felt. Hans and Marta looked at each other and shared knowing eyes. It was clear to them how trying today was proving for their parish priest.

'Good morning,' she said simply before removing her gloves and placing them inside her handbag. Her auburn hair was beautiful, Marta noticed almost shyly.

'Mrs Beck,' Father Maier greeted, with Marta listening keenly to catch the name. 'So very good to see you... very good,' he said.

To the side of them, Marta smiled awkwardly, waiting for the right moment to say hello and to join the conversation. She shifted her handbag so that it rested on one arm, leaving one hand free to shake their new companion's hand. Hans stood a pace back. Marta tried not to be irritated.

'Mrs Richter,' Marta said by simple way of introduction, shaking Mrs Beck's hand lightly. 'And my husband Hans.'

Hans stepped forward, smiling, and shook Mrs Beck's hand, offering a warm hello. No "Heil Hitlers".

A brief pause, during which the woman in crimson pulled out of her handbag a silver holder and elegantly lit a cigarette. She politely offered Marta and Hans one, but neither accepted as Father Maier took a step back from the party, and a breath. *Have faith*, his mind repeated.

'Ladies… Hans,' he said, amid gentle smiles among the group.

The woman in crimson thought it only polite to stub out her cigarette, underneath her heel, as he started speaking. Marta could not help but watch her, wishing she enjoyed her confidence.

'Let us depart, or we will be late… and we don't want to be late,' Father Maier said spiritedly and the four of them began walking, cautiously and then purposefully, away from church. Hans remained on the fringes of the group, at its back and alone with his thoughts, quietly wishing he was at home, smoking a cigarette clandestinely while his wife's eyes were elsewhere, and reading his newspaper. He crossed his legs in those moments. *Luxury*, he pined, before shaking off the daydream and picking up his pace, walking beside his wife, who was grateful for not having to look over her shoulder. She glanced across briefly at his presence and she was comforted. She watched their feet walk in perfect time and she smiled, like she was someone younger. She felt his eyes on her.

Marta and Mrs Beck were soon walking side by side on the pavement, both having chosen to sport their flat weekend heels for comfort. Father Maier hovered behind them clumsily, which they were both amusingly aware of. He was fussing over his collar, an old tick he thought he had forgotten, until today.

It's no good, he thought.

'Let us walk in the road,' he said, taking the lead himself. 'This is a march... it is important we are seen,' he added, as if he was airing his thoughts.

Marta and Mrs Beck exchanged playful eyes and were on the brink of smiling openly before the four of them dutifully took to the centre of the street, passing onlookers with slight unease on both sides. People wondered what they were doing. It was a Sunday. Why weren't they in church? *Why wasn't Father Maier in church?*

National Socialist flags flew overhead like sentinels, billowing on gusts of wind. Without thought, Father Maier picked up his stride until he really was marching.

'Father, please...' Marta politely complained from behind. 'I am afraid my legs aren't quite as young as yours.'

Father Maier closed his eyes and opened them, and immediately regained his sense of temper.

'Of course,' he said. 'I am sorry, Mrs Richter.'

'Thank you.' Marta smiled and the four of them continued happily on their way.

'What brings you here today?' Marta then asked Mrs Beck, above the polite tap of their heels, surprising herself with the directness of her question.

Before replying, Mrs Beck lit a cigarette. 'Would you like one?' she asked Marta.

'No... no,' Marta said. 'Maybe in my twenties... I gave up a long time ago, when I was pregnant with my daughter.'

Mrs Beck nodded while continuing to smoke her cigarette and enjoy its smoky blooms fogging her head. As they spoke and walked, Marta felt the curious eyes of onlookers on them. Sensing a pause, she looked briefly at her new acquaintance, who squinted as smoke rising from her cigarette stung one of her eyes. Marta did not quite know what to make of her and looked forward once again, and wiped her hair, buffeted by the wind, out of her face.

Marta wanted to confide in Mrs Beck but felt it best to keep her eyes fixed forward, unless invited otherwise by her companion. Failing to felt voyeuristic somehow. She wished she could put her finger on it.

She said, glancing down, 'My granddaughter, Meike, was taken to Hadamar… against her wishes… against *our* wishes. We haven't been able to go and visit her, check she is okay… just see her. I can't bear it, not knowing.'

Mrs Beck decided to finish her cigarette, tossing it underfoot while they walked forward. They passed three men, well dressed and smoking outside a coffee house, laughing too loudly for a Sunday. The men looked in their direction, Marta flushing with embarrassment.

'Don't mind them,' Mrs Beck hushed, leaning into Marta. 'They're men… that's all. Maybe they are as afraid as we are, Mrs Richter. Men just show it differently, that's all. I'm tired of being afraid, Mrs Richter… aren't you?' she said, more in statement.

Above them, the sun dipped behind clouds. All that was left was grey.

'Actually, that isn't strictly true,' Mrs Beck said. 'I am ashamed of what I've done, Mrs Richter.'

Marta frowned briefly before instinctively saying, 'I am sure you have nothing to be ashamed of.'

'That is kind, Mrs Richter,' she said before hunting back in her bag for her cigarettes.

Marta noticed with a further frown, which she instantly regretted, and Mrs Beck was self-conscious suddenly. There was a pause, which made Hans turn his head to check if his wife was okay. She felt his look, but kept her eyes fixed down.

Mrs Beck began again. 'I left my son, Mrs Richter,' she said. 'My husband and I moved to South Africa. It must have been a year after Hitler became Chancellor. My husband was terribly worried. He is a quarter Jewish, from his grandparents. I told him to stop being so ridiculous, but he wouldn't be persuaded. He hasn't come back… how right he was,' Mrs Beck said mockingly, but it was not clear towards whom. She read the question on Marta's face. 'We couldn't take Wolfgang when we left. The law had changed and forbid it. Our son is schizophrenic, Mrs Richter. He was registered. He could be…' she said, searching, 'violent. He was always so sorry afterwards.' She allowed her words to linger like smoke from her cigarette. 'We do not have relatives here in Germany,' she said. 'So, we paid for a guardian to care for Wolfgang. I never liked her, but my husband never really cared. He wanted out of Germany. He was afraid, Mrs Richter. He just didn't want to show it, like that would be enough to get him sent to a work camp. We were both running, you see, just in different directions.'

Marta tried to take Mrs Beck's words in. They were a lot, but she didn't want her expression to bely her feelings again.

'You've found your son now? You live together again?' Marta asked.

'Wolfgang was taken into care, into hospital, while we were in South Africa. Like your granddaughter, I imagine,' Mrs Beck said, borrowing Meike's experience without invitation and yet, here, with her, Marta's feelings were not offended. 'We were informed by letter, by his guardian, after the fact. We had no say.'

Marta glanced to her right and she caught Mrs Beck's eyes in hers for a moment. She offered a small smile.

Mrs Beck continued, 'My husband said, "There is war again. He's in the safest place." But I don't know if he really believed that. I knew after that, that I had to return to Germany. It had been over between us for a time, if either of us was being honest. I think both of us were glad of the excuse. Neither of us has sought a divorce,' she said, rolling the outside of a finger delicately up her eyelashes.

'Do you know currently where your son is a patient?' Marta said as the group turned into a quieter, residential street and Marta felt more comfortable. Fewer prying eyes.

'Just before I left South Africa, we received a letter from Wolfgang's guardian informing us he had been transferred to a work camp, location unknown, in Poland. His condition in hospital had become acute,' Mrs Beck said. 'He could more purposefully serve the Reich by working... it had been decided. *That* was the best course of treatment.'

Marta nodded, deciding it was safest to say nothing in reply for the moment.

'I have no idea where he is,' Mrs Beck said, casting her face up briefly to blink back a tear. Marta felt uncomfortable. 'He's in the wind, as my grandfather used to say.'

A pause at first between the pair grew into a silence. They both shared a smile of discomfort, catching each other's eyes awkwardly. Then, rain, rather heavy, started to fall and saved them. Marta pulled her head scarf thickly over her hair and Mrs Beck did likewise, tucking her hair in tightly.

'May I join you?' a voice said and Mrs Kohler, Horst's mother, appeared, flanking Marta and Mrs Beck.

Marta nodded gladly. What had felt like intimate company now felt like a gathering. The change of sense was significant, and the mood happily lightened.

'You may, of course. Glad to see you, Mrs Kohler,' said Marta.

'Erna, please,' she said, despite the now driving rain, making her scrunch her eyes against it.

'This is Mrs Beck,' Marta said.

'Very nice to meet you,' Mrs Beck said, offering her hand. 'And it's Eva,' she added, before hoisting a large umbrella over their heads, which the three of them quickly shared, huddling together and giggling nervously as they did so. Years fell away for a few moments.

'Erna's son was at Hadamar,' Marta said quietly, and smiles fell diplomatically from faces. Nobody said anything and Marta feared she had overstepped herself while wiping rain from her brow. It wasn't her story to tell.

'Horst, my son, died at Hadamar,' Erna said with an odd brightness before smiling at Marta in one of the kindest gestures Marta could recall. Nobody said anything as the rain and wind continued to slap the group in the face with its weight. Rain drops ran down the ends of everyone's noses. Hans checked behind him with a smirk, knowing his wife hated the elements, pulling his hat down over his head to fix it more securely, while Father Maier walked unprotected without a hat or a coat. He looked drowned and more foolish than any of them had seen him before.

Mrs Beck gave in to her habit and pulled a cigarette from her case in her handbag. She immediately failed and then failed again to light it during the downpour. Marta and Mrs Kohler noticed, and couldn't help but share a smile, conspiratorial schoolgirls once more. Mrs Beck then realised. She looked across at the two of them and, for the briefest moment, Marta thought it was going to end badly before the three of them erupted into loud laughter. Hans and Father Maier cast a look back, over their shoulders.

Mrs Beck, at the heart of the trio, then locked arms with Mrs Kohler, flanking her to one side and Marta to her other. The warmth of each of them was welcome against the wet and even if only for a second, the small act represented something greater.

'I've never liked a man in a moustache,' Mrs Beck said, with the beginnings of a smile, raising her head high in spite of the rain, refusing to relent. A final look of confirmation between the three of them before laughter, more natural now, warmed each of them, including Hans and Father Maier, steadfastly out front and leading the walking party. Then, a small wonder, magical in every way the world could still be. A gang of women, five or six, almost too many to count, stood waiting for them outside the local school gates. They approached and, amid knowing nods and murmurs of greetings and hellos, they joined them on their walk, now fast reaching the city's final outskirts. Soon, open fields before Hadamar itself. Father Maier resumed the lead at the head of the pack, and he deliberately looked around, walking backwards briefly and completing a full circle, smiling. He clasped his hands together.

Have faith, he reminded himself, looking forward once more and bringing his head up to the heavens.

48

A black car, National Socialist flags in miniature fluttering on the bonnet, drove up to Hadamar hospital's grand entrance with a hum. The two soldiers on duty outside the institution's front looked uncertain.

'I am here on the wishes of Reichsführer Himmler,' the SS officer said, without looking up as he exited the vehicle, his driver holding the door open for him. The young soldiers said nothing.

A sharp knock at Devil No.1's office door.

'Enter,' Hadamar's chief doctor said, lost in paperwork at his desk.

'Dr Vogel... Heil Hitler,' a man said, entering the space and casually performing the ubiquitous salute with a seasoned flip of his wrist. He carefully removed his officer's hat as Devil No.1 rose to his feet, surprised. The Party had not informed him of an official visit. The man before him swept his hair over to one side in a rehearsed movement. He rested his hat underneath one arm. The doctor could not read him.

'Can I offer you a drink, Officer?' Devil No.1 said,

walking from his desk to a drinks cabinet, too large, the officer noted, for an office this size.

The doctor had his back to the room's window, which overlooked flat, green grounds. He was unsure if he was about to be congratulated or condemned.

'SS Officer Kramer. I am here this morning on behalf of SS Reichsführer Himmler,' he said, eyes cast aside slightly, like he was evading someone invisible in the room. 'I don't drink on duty,' he interjected, and the doctor withdrew his hand holding out a generous glass of schnapps.

Devil No.1 shrugged mentally and proceeded to pour himself a drink, looking out of his office window and finding his eyeline drawn to a tree branch, at the end of its influence. He savoured the taste of alcohol momentarily.

'How can I help?' he said.

'I have a letter to deliver, personally from Reichsführer Himmler,' the officer said, revealing and holding up a white envelope. 'It details how you will terminate all activity here at Hadamar, liquidate all evidence of what has been done here. *All* evidence. There will be nothing for anyone to discover.'

The doctor failed to absorb what he was being told. He could not prevent his head scrambling vainly to calculate whether this was good or bad for him. The officer remained silent, not wishing to say anything further, instead observing as the doctor drained his schnapps and proceeded to light a cigarette. He did offer his guest one.

The superior officer mentally summarised what he had found here: a drunk practising medicine, in the loosest terms, on cripples. His mind was soon filled with desire to leave, return to Berlin and prepare for meetings he had later today.

'Reichsführer Himmler was not happy when I left him last night,' the officer spoke.

Devil No.1 inhaled the last of his cigarette hurriedly and retreated to the chair behind his desk.

'All the details are here,' the officer said, placing the envelope down on the desk so the doctor had to reach to retrieve it. 'They are quite... simple,' he said, allowing the last word to hang on his lips like an unsolicited kiss. The officer turned his back on the doctor and surveyed himself the view from the office window. He continued, 'There was an incident. A Sunday. A local priest led a small march to this... *your* hospital,' the officer said like a surgeon taking pride in making so few incisions on a patient. 'News has spread,' the officer said, choosing to fix his hat back smartly on his head. 'You understand?'

Devil No.1 rose to his feet, quiet fury creeping up his face but with no outlet here. He began fixing himself a second drink. Paperwork could wait. He knew the day was already a write-off.

'It was a minor incident,' the doctor then said, keeping his back to the officer. 'My guards informed me it was no more than ten people.'

'My' guards, the officer's imagination complained. But what else had he expected to find here? It was not a question.

'It does not matter,' the officer said. 'If those ten people each tell ten others, and they then... you understand,' he said once more, drawing the debate to a close like he was cleaning his knife of blood, ready for the next operation.

In the pause, the two of them made eye contact for the first time. The doctor was first to pull his gaze, turning away and blinking rapidly, like when he was anxious as a boy.

49

Alfred stood in his usual spot, at the fence bordering Hadamar's grounds. He lifted his head slowly following his constant prayer, asking God for Meike to be here. He looked up and he opened his eyes, scanning the grounds and patients out today greedily. Meike wasn't among them and his head, like his spirits, immediately dropped. Alfred stomached the disappointment, breathing through his nose and looking up, taking in the universally grey sky, so monotone and unfeeling, like there could be nothing magical like the moon or the stars beyond.

It was Friday and normally, at the end of the week, he would hurry home after the day's final lesson, but something in him couldn't face doing so today. His pull towards Meike was like the tide and yet, in his heart, she only felt further away from him, drifting out in the ocean somewhere.

Alfred gripped the wire with renewed frustration. He tilted his head up and he breathed. He looked ahead once more, and his eyes were quickly drawn to a tall girl he did not overly recognise from the usual suspects he spotted each day. She was thin like a rake and pushing a fellow patient in a wheelchair, but it was not Meike. He sighed. His mother would be beginning to wonder where he was. *Eight. Nine. Nearly there. Ten. Then chaos.*

The thud of a vehicle in the distance, buffeting angrily over the potted road which led up to the hospital front. It sounded like a large vehicle. Alfred raced towards the noise like a hare, drawn increasingly to the chatter of teenagers. He ran and his senses were greeted by the sound of adult authority ordering the group loudly off the bus. It was a bus. *A bus.* He hadn't seen one since the day he had first had the idea.

The easiest way into Hadamar was not through some hole in the fence, of a neglected corner of the hospital grounds. It was right through the front door.

50

Alfred pulled the slack of his satchel tight on his back. He had water and a chunk of chocolate he was saving for the journey back home. Through the mess of bodies congregating outside Hadamar, he safely navigated his way to the blind side of the bus, opposite to where its cargo of teenagers were still being unloaded by soldiers. He stood there gasping for a moment. The soldiers' voices were close, frighteningly close. Alfred tried to collect himself. He couldn't believe how brave he was being. Or stupid. Fear deafened his senses from every angle.

Suddenly, he felt himself being heaved up off his feet by a granite-like grip, which had lassoed hold of his satchel on his back and was manhandling him, at the back of a growing line of other teenagers now entering the building. No way out now. *Eight. Nine. Nearly there.*

Alfred was then surprised again, this time by himself. Standing claustrophobically in line and being buffeted by other teenagers, either stony silent or excitedly loud, he began to quietly cry, tears creeping down his cheeks like the first crack in a dam. He coughed up increasing releases of emotion. He felt small, glancing up the flight of stairs, underlining Hadamar's portentous doors.

'Quickly, quickly!' a soldier shouted and a boy in front of Alfred, who he thought did not look disabled, received a jolt in his back, jarring him forward. Alfred did not understand. Why wasn't there a rich gallery of life limping ahead, aided by an array of wonderful contraptions? But nothing. Just youngsters. Like him, scared, uncertain and cowering if a soldier raised a hand or a rifle to them. Alfred's instincts were on acute alert. *Eight. Nine. Nearly there. Ten. Then chaos.*

'Quickly!' a soldier boomed in Alfred's ear, causing him to shrink a little closer to the earth. 'Quickly… idiot!' the voice elongated with relish and the line of teenagers lurched forward until it was Alfred's turn to climb the first concrete step leading up to the doors of the hospital itself. Amid the maelstrom, encircling his senses like wolves, Alfred forgot how to put one foot in front of the other, his right foot snagging the first step and stumbling his frame forward and knocking the boy in front of him. Alfred felt a thick slap across the back of his head which immediately began to throb.

'Idiot!' a voice yelled and Alfred feared he might cry again, but, to his relief, he didn't. He managed to move his feet up the flight of steps and he was only a few feet from the entrance. He would be inside. He prayed he'd made the right decision.

Once a few feet inside, Alfred could see up ahead, towards the front of the queue of teenagers patiently in line. A nurse checked someone's hair before funnelling them forward with an unforgiving start and a final stumble into the real belly of the building. Alfred watched another nurse walking up and down the line of teenagers, surveying them. *She's the only nurse not carrying a clipboard*, Alfred tried to mentally note, despite a thumping heart in his chest.

'Good afternoon and welcome to Hadamar,' the nurse began, turning around each time she reached the end of the line, only to walk hypnotically back up it. 'Where you will remain for the rest of the war. Today, you are useless... worthless to the Reich. It is our job here to discover which of you may be worthy and in future, be able to contribute to society.'

Alfred successfully began to slow his breathing, as he focused on the nurse's welcome message. The corridor where they stood didn't look to Alfred like a hospital corridor. He did not know what to make of that, but his instincts were telling him loudly that he only had himself to rely upon now. Alfred's focus switched, with a turn of his head, to a girl crying behind him in line. He could only catch her face fleetingly. He dare not look around fully. The girl's crying became worse, and Alfred was worried of the repercussions, for her and them all.

The lead nurse stopped pacing up and down the line, and she stood alongside the crying girl, half a step behind so she was not quite parallel.

'Could I get your parents?' the nurse asked the girl. 'Your father, perhaps? Or mother? Would you like that?'

'Yes,' the girl sobbed. 'Yes.'

'They... are... not... coming,' the nurse whispered in her ear before turning her voice back up to full volume. 'Your parents consented to you coming here. They don't want you as you are,' the nurse said and the girl stopped crying.

Nobody made a sound as they all slowly shuffled forward, in readiness for waiting nurses to roughly check their hair for lice, Alfred saw, tilting his head to gain a view of what was happening, what he was about to face. Afterwards, he noticed each teenager was handed a bar of soap and a white towel. They were asked to strip to their underwear and to form a new line hugging the corridor's opposite wall. Boys and girls were present.

A snigger. Met with a slap across the back of a head, silencing it and any seditious thoughts of adding to it. Eyes dropped forward staring at bare feet. Alfred was still waiting for his hair to be checked, stood on wooden floorboards, liable to creak underfoot like landmines. Anyone unfortunate enough to set one off was met with a clipboard thumping the back of their head. More of the youngsters were stifling quiet sobs now.

A nurse startled Alfred and began coarsely checking through the hair of the boy in front of him, like he was subversively hiding something up there. Alfred could only listen in stereo to aggressive jabs of the nurse's hands and fingers, alongside helpless complaints from the boy. Any resistance was followed by a sharp slap and Alfred braced himself to remain absolutely still when it was his turn. It soon was.

The nurse's hands yanked rudely his head this way and that, abruptly tilting it. Alfred felt his neck jar under the shocks of movement. He closed his eyes and began to try to separate his body from his mind. It felt weird in the darkness, experiencing the assault to his hair in almost complete submission. Time began to shift to a new rhythm and Alfred succeeded in not making a sound. The ordeal was over. *Eight. Nine. Nearly there.* From the nurse, Alfred accepted a bar of soap like cold clay and a fresh towel. He could feel his mind revolting against the circumstance. The longer Alfred spent here, the closer he came to danger. His mind fought an urge to turn and run, run like the wind out of this place, out of here, and to never look back. But he couldn't. Alfred didn't.

He had come here for Meike. She *was* here and she had been here for weeks now. What had she suffered during all that time? Alfred's imagination could not answer, but he was appreciating it can't have been good. She needed his help. She needed him. He just needed to find her. *Eight. Nine. Nearly there. Ten.*

Then chaos.

51

Pinching, pulling, pushing, Alfred felt each assault of his limbs intimately. A nurse was grabbing his arms and roughly removing his school shirt. A shirt button pinged to the floor and Alfred heard it dance on the wood floor below. Alfred tried once more to remove his mind from the situation, but being undressed by an adult woman was more disturbing, more difficult. Alfred found his mind giving in and he watched her fail to make eye contact with him like he was subhuman. She slapped him crassly on the back of his head and he attempted to cease all struggle in each of his limbs. His head stung. He was a teenage boy, and this was a grown woman. The distaste in his mouth curdled like off milk.

Alfred surprised himself at how immediately hardened he was becoming to this process, whatever *it* was. Had this hardness been hidden in him all his life? He glanced down, amid the tornado in miniature enveloping him, and he kneaded wooden floorboards with his bare feet and toes. The sharpness of his senses was like pins. *Eight. Nine. Nearly there.*

All the new patients stood in line, stripped of their previous selves and semi-naked in only underwear, quietly holding soap and a towel. Their heads were submissively lowered, eyes fixed downcast on the heels of the person in front. Everyone's skin was breaking out into red rages from where the nurses had clawed them. Most were past crying. Alfred realised how cold he was, running a finger over large goose bumps populating his naked arms and legs. He tried to hold himself in to stay warm, but it wasn't really helping. He was too exposed. They all were. A girl with auburn hair stood in front of Alfred in the line and she was breaking the tacit silence, weeping openly. Alfred turned his head and looked out the corner of his eyes. He could not see a nurse nearby. They had been left alone briefly.

'It's okay,' he said, placing a hand like a butterfly on the girl's cold arm in front. She jumped at his touch and span her head around before realising it was benign. Alfred had always had a kind face. She tried to smile back, but the experience was overwhelming. Alfred smiled sadly and he knew it best to leave her be and let her deal with what was happening in her own way. If the roles had been reversed, that's what Alfred would have wanted, wondering what lay waiting for them. *Eight. Nine. Nearly there.*

52

The fresh intake of patients was walking into a dressing room of sorts, filled with wooden benches. The floor was frozen like ice, forcing Alfred and the others to pick their feet up like they were dancing on hot potatoes.

'Remove your underwear,' a nurse said, and she was instantly met with paralysed refusal from every teenager. The group had still not been split by sex. Teenage glances crisscrossed the group. Making the first move seemed unthinkable.

'Remove your underwear,' the nurse said, and youngsters obeyed in slow motion, shuffling pants uncomfortably down naked legs until there was nothing left. Only themselves, which they each held awkwardly, protecting what dignity they could. Alfred hung onto his vest the longest before removing it in a final forced movement.

'If any of you idiots… you little perverts look at another patient while showering, you will sleep outside in your nightshirt… on bare ground,' she said with a plainness which persuaded each teenager she meant it.

'There is nothing here to see here,' she continued playfully. 'All idiots here… idiot boy… idiot girl.'

Alfred imagined her speaking to Meike in this way and he could not help but eyeball her out of the corner of his eye. He closed his eyes to try and contain his anger, and he stood perfectly still, naked, with only a bar of soap and a white towel in his possession. Wow, he was cold. *Eight. Nine. Nearly there.*

'Follow the idiot in front of you,' the nurse said, continuing to hold court.

The teenagers queued, heads bowed, the shock now of being nude, in front of one another, having left them on some level. Soft skin kissed cold concrete as bare, teenage feet shuffled forward into the communal shower.

'Leave your towel where you are. Collect it afterwards,' the nurse said. 'Keep your bar of soap, keep following the idiot in front of you,' she commentated as Alfred reached his turn to come within touching distance of her, before filing underneath the rows of shower heads and raining water falling down from the shower heads above.

'Maybe there is hope for German women yet,' she said, eyes running up and down Alfred's frame. 'If only you didn't have idiot genes in your young balls,' she mimicked like a monkey and Alfred thought he heard Polish in her accent. He badly wanted the ordeal to end. He wanted to be reunited with his shoes and his clothes and then he could better decide what to do. He continued to walk forward, head down and unflinching, following the back of female calves and pretty heels in front of him. Even here, he could not help but find them attractive.

Jesus Christ! his head cursed, as he walked into what felt like a wall of ice and making him curl into himself. Exposed under the large shower heads, pouring out painfully cold water, it was useless, like Hadamar had discovered how to forge water from iron. As they showered, patients cried out at varying volumes. Only the odd one remained muted.

'Quiet!' cried the nurse.

Do something, Alfred, his head urged, peering down at his shaking hands, which he willed to hastily rub soap over frozen skin. He looked forward through the frozen waterfall and he recognised the heels of the girl in front of him. He nudged her as politely as he could. She had stopped moving as if she had become frozen under the barrage. At least the gush of shower heads offered their conversation cover.

'Come on! We have to get out of here,' Alfred hushed. They brushed bare arms and Alfred felt her goose bumps on his own. 'We have to move,' he whispered again, and she looked back at him and finally began to move forward out of the shock of water.

Alfred soon stood rapidly towelling his arms and chest to try and reintroduce some feeling back into his body, which had started to turn blue. The more he rubbed, the more he began to shiver. *Eight. Nine. Nearly there.*

53

In the hospital corridor, Alfred stood in line with the others, gladly wearing once more his white underpants and vest. Alfred held himself tightly and he quietly rubbed his body to try and warm it without drawing attention. He stood opposite double doors in a large corridor populated by meagre apparatus. Occasionally, nurses hurried past.

The double doors bloomed open, surprising Alfred, and a man wearing a white coat walked through with the gait of a friend's mother after drinking schnapps during the day. The man smiled when he saw the teenagers.

'Afternoon... ladies and gentleman,' he said, opening his hands theatrically. 'And welcome to Hadamar. I hope you enjoy your time with us. All clean and spick and span, I see,' he said, walking up and down the line of new hospital patients. Alfred trained his eyes on him.

'Yes, Doctor,' said the nurse who had made them shower. 'All ready. Their clothes are being processed.'

Alfred watched another nurse appear through the double doors the doctor had emerged from, pushing a large laundry cart spilling out with clothes, presumably from other patients, Alfred thought, folding his elbows tight against his sides. The doctor then stopped and peered at Alfred, who did not lift his eyes to meet the doctor's the entire time. *Keep your head down, head down, Alfred.*

He released a breath when he heard the man's footsteps pace away on the corridor floor before the doctor continued speaking in a more sober tone.

'The next stage of the process, of becoming a new patient at Hadamar, is an inoculation, a small jab.' He lingered. 'To protect you from disease from idiots who have already joined us.'

Alfred listened to the words, but he was no longer hearing them. All he could focus on was how cold he still was. He wished he could shake the feeling off, which seemed to be cloaking him like a cape. He needed to get warm, he decided, otherwise he could not think clearly about what to do next. He looked down and he saw his big toe, on one foot, squashed slightly from a rock he had lifted on a beach when he was little, before summarily dropping to see what would happen. Why had he done that? His memory could only recall flashes, nothing longer to answer his question.

His attention shifted. The girl with the pretty heels stood shaking in front of him, shuddering with her teeth quietly clacking. Alfred willed her to be quiet.

'Doctor,' a nurse called and the man in the white coat paced away from the line of fresh teenage patients, the nurse from the showers following him and leaving them unattended suddenly. Alone. Alfred's senses crackled like a firefight. Was this his chance? *Eight. Nine. Nearly there.*

Alfred span his head around, frantically scanning up and down the corridor for any sign of authority. In the distance and over the heads of other patients, he could see the fading light reaching through the hospital entrance, which opened back out into green countryside. The light was soon swallowed by a dimness which seemed to pervade Hadamar completely. Temptation coursed through Alfred like adrenaline.

He continued to look about nervously and to rapidly assess his options. He had to go. Did he? Yes? No? His mind raced to decide. He took a first sideways step left, out into the middle of the dim corridor, darkening now with the beginnings of dusk, creeping in from outside like vines.

Stepping out closer to the heart of the large corridor felt significant. Nothing bad happened to him after doing so. He frantically checked all around where he stood once more, feeling like everyone and no one was studying him intently. And yet nothing, nobody. *Go*, Alfred's head then urged. *Go*.

54

In measured steps, Alfred paced forward before shifting through the gears and breaking out into a controlled run. Some teenagers, all still obediently hugging the large corridor's wall, became vocalised as Alfred broke clear of them and disappeared deeper into the hospital. Wooden flooring creaked in complaint beneath Alfred's bare feet, moving too quickly now to care where they were placed. Alfred was afraid the small commotion would draw attention and end his bid to find Meike before it had begun. He did not feel so afraid now he was assuming control of the situation, sparks of movement warming his frame and limbs once more. The experience was intoxicating. Alfred could feel everything. A nurse. *A nurse!* Heading this way. Alfred instinctively dived down a short corridor. A dead end, bar the thin skeleton of a hospital cart he could crouch behind.

He huddled still as impatient footsteps, irregular in pace, grew louder. Alfred, his heart thumping in his breast, tried to even think himself small and did not dare look up as the nurse passed. And she did. *She has!* The success, however small, was exhilarating.

Alfred stretched himself back up and crept to the hospital's main corridor, and looked up and down it. Nobody. He continued his progress deeper into the belly of the building. Every foot forward represented a step further from home, a step he would have to remake were he and Meike to safely make it out of here. She had to be this way.

Alfred tiptoed down the corridor, staying light on his feet, both emboldened and fearful at every breath. Any moment could be his last. Human traffic, up ahead. Nurses, it appeared, mainly, scuttling left and right at a junction cutting across the main corridor. A ward with Meike on could be off any one of these turnings, but it was too dangerous to walk any closer. Alfred had to hide for now.

He stopped where he was, momentarily exposed and turning around to assess his surroundings. He was still wearing only a vest and his underwear, which occasionally glinted white in the growing gloom. He looked back over his shoulder and in the distance, he saw two soldiers heading this way. *You can't stay here, Alfred.* He ducked down the next short, thin corridor, which led to two rooms either side at its walled end. He stepped forward slowly, deliberately, his bare feet able to travel silently on what were no longer wooden floorboards, but what looked like a newer surface. He peered around one of the two doors. It was ajar and it felt to Alfred like his safest option, compared to risking opening the other door.

Alfred reached his head forward as much as he could into the room. No one. He breathed deeply. Voices behind him ramped tension up in his body. Alfred held his breath and he tried to think. *Hide*, he urged himself.

Alfred surveyed the space he occupied as quickly as he could, flicking his eyes left and right, up and down. Voices, louder and louder, interrupted his increasingly panicked thought process. His time was almost up. Alfred instinctively dashed to the back of the room and crouched down low behind a body of large linen baskets. Two voices now, terrifyingly close. Alfred felt they could hear him breathe.

His heart seemed to stop beating briefly and Alfred feared in the endless silence that it might actually explode. It ached painfully in his chest. The sound of the voices peaked and Alfred felt their resonance almost reach into the room before finally, finally, growing quieter and heading deeper into the hospital away from where he hid. Safe. Again. For now. Adrenaline drained from Alfred as he slipped into sleep.

*

Five. *No, six. Yes, six, surely. Blast*, thought Alfred. He had lost count. *Meike. Focus, Alfred*, he urged himself through clenched fists.

Seven. Weathered floorboards creaked beneath his feet and Alfred looked down, careful to move in case he triggered more complaints from the Richter house he was creeping through, unannounced. Alfred's head was almost in plea to the surroundings.

Eight. Nine. This was it. *Nearly there.* Ahead on the wall, Alfred could make out the beginnings of the door to Meike's room. *Ten. Ten,* Alfred repeated in his head for confirmation. Then chaos. Loud banging outside. *What on earth?* Alfred froze, like the violent sound had paralysed him where he stood, trapped in the corridor. He dare not antagonise it further.

Loud banging anew. God, was it his mother? Or worse, his father? *How had they known I would be here?* his head raced, asking so many questions it was impossible to answer all of them.

'Meike Steinmann? We are here for Meike Steinmann. Open up... open up!' a voice demanded outside. A crack of light, inviting him forward out of the black. *Meike.*

'Alfred, Alfred!' she urged, perched in her chair and peeping out into the corridor. 'Come in, come in!'

Alfred followed and in the next breath they were suddenly together in her room, lit kindly by a bedside lamp. Nothing for a moment, only silence between them. Teenagers on the brink and yet that was forgotten now. They looked at each other. They were scared. This was not the midnight meeting either of them had dreamt of.

Alfred's eyes searched Meike's for answers, but none were forthcoming. He had only seen her confident before now. Their eyes flicked to the door of the room as they heard footsteps hurry downstairs. The front door of the house opened. Heavy footsteps travelled towards them.

'Anselma... Anselma!' a voice said. Marta's. 'Come away from there.'

Alfred and Meike looked at each other. An electric fear crackled between them.

'They are looking for Meike, Grandmother,' they heard Anselma say, and Alfred looked at Meike, whose face was horrified. A sob escaped her mouth before, with the clasp of her hand, she held it in with a final determination.

Hastily, she pushed past Alfred, who immediately moved and watched as she opened her wardrobe doors and began tossing things out. *What is she doing?*

'Get in, Alfred,' she said, spinning back around, but he didn't move. 'Get in, Alfred,' she said slowly, blowing her eyes up at him.

'Okay,' he said, ducking forward awkwardly and crouching down low beneath the rails of clothes, which stroked the top of his head and shoulders. He fought an immediate instinct to climb back out, but he trusted her. She closed the wardrobe door behind him and attempted a final smile. The two of them shared a look before the lights went out on their world.

Meike hid her fear as best she could from Alfred and from herself, spinning back around in her chair in the centre of her bedroom. It was hopeless. There was nothing she could do. She found her subconscious taking pictures in her head of her favourite things. Behind her, Alfred crouched awkwardly in darkness, holding himself tightly and listening only to the shallowness of his breath. Then.

'Meike Steinmann? Meike Steinmann!' a voice repeated, not asking now.

Silence.

'Meike Steinmann, you are ordered to come with us, on the authority of the Party. You have been assigned to a centre to care for you for the remainder of the war.'

Alfred dare not move and he found his mind willing the voice away with all its might. A new pause before Alfred heard it filled with something he instinctively never wanted to hear again. Meike. Crying.

Alfred heard a scuffle and he held on tightly to his knees, as if the wardrobe's bottom, his tiny sanctuary from this invasion, could disappear beneath him and send him spinning, falling down a black hole for all time. Alfred gripped himself harder and harder, but his hands kept slipping and losing their grip, like Meike's fading hold on freedom. Now, against her will, Alfred heard her being taken. In the moment, he made a promise.

'Leave the girl alone... leave her alone!' Alfred heard Marta yell before sounds of a fresh struggle, more disturbing in their disconnect from Alfred's blinded senses. A slap. And a shocked breath. Then silence, only silence.

Footsteps in military formation outside and car doors opening and closing. Business-like. Then a voice, more human.

'You should be ashamed of yourselves,' Marta cried out. 'She's just a girl... a girl,' she said before sobs overwhelmed her. Marta fought them and made a final dash after her granddaughter, placed in the back of a vehicle, but officers held her at arm's length. 'We'll come find you, my darling... your grandfather, your sister and I... we will come for you and visit and bring you your things,' Marta shouted, forcing her voice over the tops of officers' heads. 'My darling... my darling girl,' she hushed, but only to herself like the saddest lullaby, watching her youngest granddaughter being driven away.

55

'What have we here then?' a woman said with practised cruelty. Alfred opened his eyes, which were sore from sleep. Blinking, he realised with small horror how careless he had been. He had fallen asleep.

'I don't know how you can look at them,' another woman's voice said. 'Can we just get them down to the other end of the hospital?'

Alfred opened his eyes wildly to help awaken his senses where he lay, curled on the floor like a foetus at the back of the room. His head remained cushioned by the flat of his hands. *Nurses*, he thought, in the room where he had fallen asleep, right here. *They are right here*.

Alfred's eyes flicked around as best they could from where he lay, which he dare not disturb for fearing of making a noise and revealing himself as a perverse stowaway, hidden within the hospital. He couldn't fathom how close he was to being uncovered. With painstaking care, he slowly lifted his frame up off of the floor, pushing his weight up silently on his elbow and then shifting it delicately onto his hip. He swept his hair over to one side with a free hand. He was wide awake now.

Alfred's hearing waited to pick up on sounds around him. He continued to slowly lift his frame up off the floor before stopping. What was he thinking? He had to stay low. It was his best hope of remaining undetected.

'Let's go,' a woman said, followed by the whirring squeak of a large linen basket being wheeled out of the room and away down the short corridor, leading back up to Hadamar's central spine. 'We'll come back for the other.'

'Okay... okay,' said the other woman. 'You have to get used to this, you know. They're just idiots. You know that?'

All the while, Alfred listened intently, trapped awkwardly on the floor between climbing up off it and remaining tight to it. He was hopelessly vulnerable. The conversation between the nurses trailed off and he breathed deeply and loudly once he felt he was safe to do so. *Blast*, Alfred admonished himself angrily, *blast*. How could he have been so careless? How could he?

Shaking his head, he stood upright, eyes still fixed in tension on the room's door, which remained glaringly open after the two nurses had exited. Alfred did not have long, perhaps, before they returned, and he could see how perilously close he had been to being discovered. Next time, he vowed, he would not be so lucky. *Meike*, he reminded himself. *Meike*.

Alfred let out another heavy breath and he tried to gather himself for what still lay ahead. He didn't know. He blinked. He did not feel good. His heart pulled for home, where he was safe with his parents. He fought through the feeling, creeping up to the room's door, which hung ajar. He was incongruously still wearing a winter coat he had commandeered before sleep had overtaken him. Underneath its long drapes, he still wore only white underwear. There was nothing covering his bare feet and legs.

Alfred peered his head out into the corridor leading up to the hospital's main thoroughfare. There was no one. Safe, for the moment. His instinct told him to head back up to the double doors he had seen the doctor appear from earlier, closer to the hospital's entrance. *Wards for patients could be through them*, he thought. Meike could be through them. His feet felt clammy on the cold floor, sneaking forward once more on the balls of his feet, ready at any notice to take flight. He hugged the side of the main corridor for what cover it could provide him before his eyes were drawn up to high ceilings and windows. Dark had settled on Hadamar like black snow.

Alfred thought that there would be fewer nurses working at night, allowing him to move about more easily. Fewer dangers, fewer chances to be seen.

He returned to the relative safety of the laundry room, which had become his temporary sanctuary, but his head was dizzy with decisions. What should he do? Should he wait until it was even later? Or should he begin searching the hospital immediately?

And what about his mother? Alfred knew from experience that she would graduate rapidly from fretting to frantic before finally driving his father mad. His father would always redirect that ire straight back at Alfred when he finally did walk back through their front door, guilty eyes cast down, hoping for the best but always fearing the worst. On those occasions, he recalled, he could forget his supper, instead dismissed to bed achingly hungry, the sensation making his night's sleep only more uneasy. By morning, eyes heavy and his body almost past the point of hunger, Alfred would trudge downstairs and wearily hope time and a night's sleep had diluted his father's indignation, his mother smiling quietly when it always had, and watching him hungrily eat the extra breakfast she had prepared for him.

My school bag. My school bag, Alfred suddenly thought, his head back in the room. It had been tossed in blindly with everyone's clothes from the busload who had arrived this afternoon. Alfred plunged his arms deep into one of the laundry baskets and he was rewarded when, finally, he successfully retrieved his bag, happily holding it aloft and peering at it like a lost friend. Alfred was amazed by the boost to his mood. He reached inside for a canteen of cold water he had filled earlier at school and which he now glugged from greedily, precious drops dripping down his chin in his haste. Alfred quickly experienced a revitalising revival, like a secret sleep, and he gasped for breath after finishing drinking. A small smile drew across his lips. He dug a hand back into his bag and he placed his fingers on chunks of dark chocolate, wrapped in used newspaper. He had been saving them for today. He was hungry and he could not resist biting the chocolate in two and savouring it in his mouth. He closed his eyes and slowed his chew like he was trying to memorise its taste. Alfred then dutifully wrapped the remaining chocolate back in the old newspaper and placed it back in his satchel for Meike, picturing a future where she would love his kindness. He took a final glug of water from his canteen and screwed the lid back on tight, then he placed it safely inside his satchel, which he clipped close.

He pulled the satchel snugly around his shoulders and he breathed loudly. He knew that he was readying himself. He had gotten this far, he told himself. Now he had to take the final steps and find Meike.

Alfred noticed a leg, pale and pink, hanging limp from one of the large laundry baskets. *A mannequin*, he thought, walking up closer to inspect it. He reached forward and touched the leg before immediately dropping it and standing still. His mind was playing tricks on him. *Surely*.

Alfred looked back at the limb and the fleshy toes at its end, empty and unloved. Their touch. He had been expecting hard plastic, but instead he had experienced a different texture. Human. He stepped back up to the large basket and he peered over it into its abyss.

He kept his mouth closed, terrified of what he would find, and looked again at the leg, examining it as best he could, sticking up from the middle of the thigh before a sea of clothing hid the rest. The large basket reached up to the bottom of Alfred's breast, which was thumping underneath the overcoat he had commandeered. His feet felt a flush of cold and stuck with each step to the floor. The limb.

Alfred kept his hands close by his side, as if the leg could be infectious. It was unmistakable now. How had he not seen? It was thin and oddly plastic, but nothing less than entirely human. Alfred began carefully removing items of clothing from the basket and lifting the lid on its jumbled contents. He did not know what he was about to uncover.

He did not need to delve very deep. And there they were, haunting, looking up at him, and yet somehow further, looking through Alfred into forever. The young corpses' eyes were hollow, as if the hospital's nurses had been ordered to remove their real ones for safekeeping and now only fake ones had been plugged in their place.

Mouths hung open, while others were closed. Alfred was transfixed briefly before regaining control of his senses. He spun away, retching and spitting out sticky chocolate his body had not had time to yet digest. His throat burnt and he rested his hands on his knees to hold himself still for a moment. Alfred looked over his shoulder once more and the bodies were still there, lifeless. They had not disappeared, instead only growing more real as Alfred submitted to his intrigue and he studied them more closely, tangled and naked, blank, gasping in their final realisation, wide eyed in that moment now captured for eternity. This was not who they were. But how did they die? *Why did they die?*

Hoots, deep within the hospital, brought Alfred out of his trance. Darkness was coming outside, enveloping everything in a portentous blue. *Home.* Alfred wanted to go home, to be home. He was so far from its sanctuary. But Meike. He had to get Meike, before it was too late.

56

Alfred was readying himself to leave the laundry room, heaving on ill-fitting and foreign trousers. He tried not to think about their owner now. He next found a pair of scuffed shoes and he tied them on tight, to compensate for them being a size too big for his feet, Alfred's toes failing to fill the shoes' ends. He found a V-neck jumper, sleeveless and wool, which soon warmed his chest beneath the coat he had found earlier and which he now pulled on over his new clothes. He instantly felt better, as if his borrowed outfit was body armour, protecting him for what he was about to attempt.

Far-off shrieks again and Alfred half turned his head to the room's door. The sound was haunting, and they reminded Alfred of where he was, where he remained. The hoots sounded to Alfred, buttoning up his long coat, like Hadamar's night-time population, whatever *it* was, was awakening and reclaiming the hospital now its daytime inhabitants were no longer present.

Alfred stood at Hadamar's main central corridor, peering up and down its long expanse, unerring and reminiscent of the road through the trees, which had grown to become Alfred's friends of late. There was nobody Alfred could now see. It was a good start.

Alfred's instincts reminded him to hug the building walls and to move quickly in the shadows, staying as light on his feet as he could, in spite of his oversized shoes, which anchored his steps clumsily like a clown. He looked down at them, willing them to behave. It was no good, Alfred decided, and he untied them and kicked them off. Bare foot, which had its downsides, but better, he felt, feeling the balls of his feet as he danced slowly forward on them. Now, he was ready.

He arrived back at the double doors he had seen the doctor emerge from all those lifetimes earlier. He placed both hands flat on them, like he was testing them for what lay beyond, and he paused before pushing them open. He walked through.

He found himself on a ward and he turned his head to the right, noticing the moon watching him navigate through the space. As he walked forward, its gaze lit up his back. Alfred wasn't sure whether the moon was his friend or his foe. He stepped quietly through what he realised, in the gloom, was a large ward filled with empty beds, unmade and unkempt, his gaze underlined by angles of moonlight slicing against the darkness.

Alfred walked carefully in between beds on either flank, breaking both rules he had set himself: he was neither hugging a wall, nor was he moving quickly. He increased his pace up the centre of the space and was increasingly certain that nobody was here. It looked like people had left in a hurry.

Alfred reached the end of the ward and was faced with another set of double doors. He looked back, over his shoulder, to survey the ground he had covered, making sure he had not missed anything, that his eyes had not betrayed him. They hadn't, he was sure. Alfred pushed a ghostly walking frame, abandoned and sat in front of the double doors, out of his way, squeaking softly on rubber wheels as he did so.

He walked through the double doors, carefully catching them so they flapped softly shut behind him. He stepped forward. Another ward, just like the one he had vacated. Nobody, again, he quickly estimated, casting his eyes across the space's surface like a net. As he did so, Alfred held his breath.

His eyes were accustomed now to the black and its shades, like a charcoal rainbow. The stark borders between moonlight and black were blurring. No one was here on this new ward. *Meike.* Where was she?

A loud bang and Alfred froze, anxiously spinning around, but nothing. The noise echoed for a moment as the building's bones seemed to creak. Alfred dashed quickly back to the hospital's main corridor, where he had come from. He felt horribly torn. His conscience nagged him that he hadn't properly explored where he had just retreated from, while his instincts argued that it was a dead end, nobody was there. He continued to listen to his instincts. They were all he had now.

Alfred walked down Hadamar's main corridor, travelling deeper into the building's belly. It felt wrong and right with every brave step he placed forward. *Meike has to be this way*, he told himself.

He saw the beginnings of lights ahead, shining in from side corridors. Light meant activity and activity meant life, people and patients. He moved closer and felt something snag his heels. The trousers he had found earlier had begun to sag. If Alfred had been startled and had tried to run, he could have tripped. Alfred bent down and he rolled up the trousers at their bottom, folding them over his exposed ankles. As he did so, he balanced himself against a large desk. Two figures were approaching. People. *People!*

It had felt so long since Alfred had seen anyone, his conscious had almost sleepwalked into danger. He was furious with himself, ducking low behind the desk before him and stooping small before two women, he recognised from their voices, nurses he assumed, strode past.

'We are injecting all remaining patients tonight,' one said. 'Only the starvation ward left to complete.'

'What will we do then?' the other asked.

'Look for new posts, I imagine,' she said, her voice fading as it travelled away from where Alfred hid tightly crouched. He stayed stooped behind the desk, his heart rate gratefully slowing again, when he noticed a carpet of papers, strewn and official looking, under his feet. Words and numbers. Equations. The National Socialist eagle perched at the top of each page, imperious, a silent witness to everything.

Alfred carefully lifted himself back to his feet, keeping watch all around in case anyone was approaching. He didn't want to be caught cold a second time. A picture of Meike's smile interrupted his imagination and he didn't know why. He was instinctively going to smile in response before remembering where he was. He shuddered.

He hugged a wall of the main corridor, mobile again, and made his way towards the increasingly bright beacon of light. He walked towards it as the disturbing hoots grew louder. He readied himself to run like the wind. The closer he stepped, the more audible the hoots became, the more human. It was people, not monsters.

Alfred began picking out individual voices as he continued to creep forward. Twenty metres, perhaps, separated him from the corridor's end and the light shining now, bright both left and right. Alfred tiptoed his way through an increasing maze of hospital apparatus, abandoned and cluttering the corridor like it was the end of the world. Papers again haphazardly carpeted the floor, reflecting moonlight in their white. Alfred hardly dare look down. Fear, white hot, lit up his chest. Alfred smelt burning.

Two figures flashed across the end of the corridor, startling Alfred, who continued to press himself tightly against the corridor wall. *What did they have on their heads?* Alfred reached the end of the main corridor and he looked to his right and into darkness. He turned to his left and witnessed light, both inviting and ominous. What would he do if he was seen? Alfred didn't know.

He pointed himself left and tried to be butterfly light on his feet. He did not have far to tread before he was able to reach his head around into a space and shocks of hot air, so intense he quickly found his body begin to prickle with perspiration. He felt achingly vulnerable.

Alfred ghosted past an open door to the space emitting throbs of heat like Berlin in early August. Alfred hid on the other side of the room's entrance, away from the main corridor. As he stole past, he could not stop himself spying a gaggle of nurses, doctors and soldiers, raising glasses and in various forms of undress. He peered around once more and he was met by the sight of a doctor pulling a nurse to him, lassoing her waist with an arm and kissing her drunkenly. He emerged from the embrace and stepped back from her, eyeing her greedily. Someone began to speak as Alfred pinned himself back to the wall. Alfred could hear intimately, which, in the moment, only seemed to amplify how reckless his position was. He closed his eyes and he focused.

'Our work here at Hadamar ends tonight,' a man said. 'And it has been important work, important enough to come to the attention of Reichsführer Himmler. History will envy us,' the man added, accompanied by drunken calls of support and then dishevelled whispers demanding quiet.

Alfred gave in to temptation and peered his head around with his back still flat on the wall outside. He quickly surveyed the group and couldn't believe what he saw. Nurses, wearing crowns of flowers on their heads, some straight, others skewed. Bottles stood tipsily at their feet, some empty, some half full. One was kicked over with a clink and rolled out of Alfred's sight until he heard it stop with a thud on the wall behind him. Too close for comfort. And then the whip of something unfurling and forcing Alfred to risk returning his eyes back over his shoulder once more. He watched the group gather at the mouth of a large oven. There was a body, and Alfred prickled with panic, remaining all the time pinned to the wall, like hanging on to a clifftop for dear life. Alfred closed his eyes.

He was fighting every instinct he had to leave this place, and never look back.

He scrunched his eyes tight as the male voice in the room began eulogising once more. Alfred was grateful for the sound and distraction.

The man said, 'This idiot is the 10,000th soul we have saved at Hadamar… saved.'

Cheers now from the gathering, and clinking of glasses, while a couple took the opportunity to kiss.

'We have saved these souls from themselves, and we are saving Germany… allowing it to be purer, fitter, and stronger as we help build a thousand-year Reich.'

Roars, raucous now, followed by shrieks and spilling glasses colliding mid-air like a dogfight. Alfred dared to look before returning to his position pinned back against the wall. The National Socialist flag was draped over the body before nurses each placed the crown of flowers from their heads on top. The sheet of metal containing the body, telltale only by exposed feet at one end, was then heaved into the furnace without ceremony and the door sliced shut to a pause and gasps, before wild laughter and gropes and gulps blurred all into one. Alfred peered around the corner again and he witnessed a nurse and a doctor, tangled together and swaying forward until they saw him. They saw Alfred.

They stopped, instantly sobered by the sight and yet unable to process it. How was it possible? The three of them stared at one other.

Alfred glanced around desperately. Silence continued, impossibly it felt, like a held breath, bursting to finally escape until Alfred's eyes widened. He bolted.

'Hey... hey!' the couple yelled as Alfred sped away, dashing into the darkness at breakneck speed. There was no chance of initially catching him.

Alfred's vision was flooded with panic. The main hospital corridor Alfred was now back on felt long and exposed, but he was running, and every thought in his intoxicated head screamed at him to put distance, more and more and more of it, between himself and the hospital officials who had spotted him. Cries behind, amplified now, shouting, demanding. Instinctively, Alfred dived off the hospital's main corridor and he burst through double doors with a gasp. He gulped in a huge breath. Another ward, much like all the others he had crept through this evening. The layout felt the same, which was a reassurance in the moment. He at least had some bearings.

He looked wildly about. He was in real danger. Voices behind him were approaching. Louder and louder. Any second now. *Any second. Move, Alfred, move*, his mind urged, and he hid low behind a bed towards the far end of the ward away from the doors, where he had entered. The doors crashed open and poured his pursuers onto the ward. They were here.

57

'Here, idiot, idiot, idiot,' a man sang into the silence before bursts of anxious laughter behind him.

'He's not an idiot,' a woman said more soberly as Alfred remained tightly crouched, tuning into their conversation from the opposite end of the ward. He reached out in the black to steady himself on bed railings and slowed his breathing before he was scared by a soft breath, much closer, making his eyes dart. He listened intently again and remained deadly still. His hunters' footsteps and voices sounded closer.

'It was a boy… I'm certain,' the woman continued to the group amid muted giggles, tipsy and disobedient. Closer, Alfred sensed, controlling his breathing like he was under water.

'Are there any patients still in here?' another woman's voice asked, and Alfred hunched even tighter into himself. That breath again. Close and soft, but real. Alfred's eyes widened to the danger, which he felt was pinning him to his position. He was trapped. He had nowhere else to run or hide. This was it.

'I can't see anything… others can finish in the morning. Then, we will be done,' a man said. They sounded so close to Alfred it felt impossible he would not be discovered.

'Come on, let's go,' a man said, and Alfred refocused, tucking his head down low once more. *Please*, a voice in his head asked.

'Come on. I need a drink,' a woman said, followed finally by footsteps moving away from Alfred. *Thank Christ.* The sound of increasingly distant laughs and exchanges was magical to Alfred's senses. They were leaving. He had survived somehow. *Thank you*, Alfred silently said in his head. A final clatter of distant doors and cries and yells, fading. Then nothing. Silence, reassuring in all its solitude.

Alfred allowed himself an audible breath and he began to slowly lift his head, looking across at the doors his pursuers had entered from. Again, nothing. Alfred was happy to mentally celebrate his success once more. He was alone and let out another breath, louder still, and unfolded himself and stood straight, releasing tension in his legs, which had been tucked all the time awkwardly beneath him. A soft breath, close again. Definite. Alfred froze.

Behind him. Someone was in the bed right behind him.

58

Alfred turned his head in slow motion, looking fearfully over his shoulder, afraid of what he was about to witness. The ward was washed in dusky blue. Alfred twisted his head and then, more bravely, his frame, and he saw a mound, unmistakably human, rise and fall beneath bed sheets. It was breathing. Alfred inched forward.

A drunk soldier, he suddenly imagined and feared, panic now prickling his skin. Alfred focused on the head peeking out from the top of the sheets cushioned by a pillow. *Blonde hair.* The beginnings of long, blonde hair. A woman. *No, a girl.* Alfred stopped and he turned his face up to the ceiling. He closed his eyes. He had found her. He had found her.

Meike.

Alfred cast his eyes forward and he reached his hand up to hold his mouth, as if it was not real, as if she was not real. *Meike.* He moved closer to her, unsure of what he was going to find, who she had become. She looked up from the darkness, like she had been sleeping. Her eyes opened and she saw him. At first, she thought she was about to touch the moon, running her fingers over its surface forged from time before time. She reached her hand up. Alfred spoke.

'Meike.' He smiled before her eyelids closed once more, leaden like the rest of her, no longer her entirely, something more, or less. Alfred was uncertain. 'Meike,' he whispered, leaning in.

She tried to respond. She was *so* tired. *Let me sleep*, her imagination sounded. *Let me sleep*.

'Meike, it's Alfred,' he said. 'Alfred... I'm here. We can go home... we're going home. Nobody will find you this time... nobody.'

He leant forward and tipped water gently from his canteen onto her lips. He poured again, more this time, as if he was tending the last plant alive on Earth, and Meike opened her eyes to Alfred's, watching, willing her. She tried to sit up, but bolts of spasms shot down her legs and instantly made her fall back flat. She was awake.

Meike blinked and she looked up at his face, and Alfred took a step back to avoid crowding her, so she could make sense of him, of this. It was real, this was happening. Meike recognised his mess of hair, which she had not been entirely in love with before. Still, it was his. Alfred was himself and she loved that about him. She smiled.

'Alfred,' she croaked, and he saw her too.

Behind them, screams echoed and Meike looked scared, folding herself into Alfred fearfully.

'We have to go,' he said.

Meike tried to take in his words and peered over to her right like a ship's passenger searching for any signs of a lifeboat. She turned to her left. Nothing. In her mind, she shook her head. It was hopeless. Where was she? Where was her friend, the girl who looked like a boy? What had they done to them?

'It's okay,' Alfred said. 'I can carry you. I can... carry you.'

But Meike only shook her head. She paused and lifted her hand too late to prevent her face from crumpling into tears. Alfred's heart broke.

Voices, loud, heading this way, and Meike and Alfred blew their eyes up at each other. No time now. A crash of double doors behind them, making Meike jump and Alfred half lean forward to stop her falling. They remained perfectly still. The voices began organising themselves. There was no time.

Meike leant into Alfred, who caught sight of her clearly for the first time in the moonlight, shining down on them from windows above. He tried not to be startled. Gaunt cheeks. And Meike's sunken eyes, which seemed to have grown larger, more fearful in the time that they had spent apart. He faked a smile.

'My chair, Alfred... we haven't got my chair,' Meike whispered.

'Keep moving! Keep moving... quickly!' a man's voice behind them. 'Check every bed... and underneath. Check everywhere... we know now. This is the last round.'

'Leave, Alfred... go!' she hushed, more urgent now. 'Go!'

No, eyes fierce and shaking his head at her, *no*.

Torchlight, shining their way.

'Hey... hey! Here!' a voice shouted followed by a rush of feet. There was no time. Panicked, Meike climbed as best she could high onto the arch of Alfred's back. Alfred lowered himself to collect her, allowing Meike to lock her hands around his neck tightly.

'You'll have to hold my feet, Alfred,' she said in his ear and he looked down at Meike's white feet and toes swinging limply, and nodded.

'Hey!' the voice cried. 'Here! Two of them.'

Alfred held the bottom of Meike's legs.

'Ready,' he said simply and Meike turned her head so the flat of her cheek was flush on his back.

'Ready,' she said.

And Alfred flew.

They startled the maze of bodies immediately ahead of them, flashing their way up the ward. Adrenaline rushed through Alfred like blood. Meike locked her fingers tightly together and she held on, scrunching her eyes shut and expecting at any second to be ripped from Alfred's back and brought crashing to the hard hospital floor.

Alfred zigzagged his way through the melee and banged loudly through the ward's double doors, voices crying after him. His thighs, built like a young bull's, burnt. His lungs were exploding.

Alfred looked up and he knew precisely where they were on Hadamar's main corridor, heading for the building's entrance. Alfred could feel Meike being buffeted violently on his back. He worried how long she could hold on.

'Stop them... stop them!' a man yelled behind them.

'Nearly there,' Alfred gasped to Meike, hanging on to him desperately. 'Nearly there,' he repeated almost silently and Meike renewed her grip around his neck.

Before them, Hadamar's main corridor was asleep in moonlight, encouraging Alfred and Meike forward.

'Oh!' Meike grimaced after one jarring footstep too many and Alfred winced anxiously.

'Nearly there,' he gasped, but he was becoming winded.

Nearly there, he urged in his head.

They were fifty yards from the hospital's main front doors. Yells and cries behind them were dulled as concentration mixed with exhaustion clouded Alfred's senses. He looked up and saw the entrance to the hospital, their salvation, closer and closer, beckoning them forward with each burning breath. He looked down at his feet and then back up again ahead at the entrance doors, and he willed them nearer, quicker than his legs could carry them. He didn't know how much longer this could continue. *Nearly there. Eight. Nine. Ten. Then chaos.*

Nothing. Like barrelling down a rabbit hole in a nightmare, falling and reaching helplessly for something, anything, to hold onto, to stop this sensation. But this wasn't some subconscious. This was real. And grave.

59

Alfred looked up from his position, prostrate on the floor. He was ten yards from the hospital entrance, which opened out onto the steps and green grounds and benign woodland which surrounded Hadamar. He looked up, panicked. *What had happened?* And Meike. Where was Meike?

'Meike, you stupid little girl,' Devil No.2 said, a slur in her voice. Meike was lying on the floor alongside Alfred, who looked at her, searching in her eyes for some indication, but he did not know what. He was uncertain. She smiled quietly at him, resigned.

Meike traced her gaze back to Hadamar's chief nurse and she considered her. Devil No.2 drank her in.

'Trying to always be everyone's friend,' she said. 'But no one has real friends.'

Meike whispered to Alfred, but he could not catch her words and he searched her eyes more explicitly for meaning, which was not forthcoming.

Hadamar's head nurse grabbed a vacant wheelchair and slammed it to the ground like it was a disobedient dog, before pacing over to Meike and hauling her up from her waist, not caring if she hurt her as she did so. Alfred hated how careless she was with her.

'Time to go, Meike,' she said, pushing forcefully down on her shoulders, as if she could fit her tightly into the chair.

Impatiently, she turned the chair around to face the long corridor heading back into Hadamar, back from where they had just run. Alfred lay still on the floor, paralysed by submission. He had failed. *He had failed.* What could he do?

'Alfred?' Meike called, but unable to fully turn as Devil No.2 pushed her away like cargo.

'Go home, young man,' Devil No.2 said. 'This place isn't for you.'

Alfred remained pinned before forcing himself to his feet. The simple act was galvanising. He watched as the chief nurse led Meike away. Meike tried to look around at him, but each time she did, Devil No.2 met her head with a slap, which hurt Alfred more than it did Meike. But it helped him. He knew now what to do. He knew what to do.

Straining briefly on the balls of his feet, Alfred sprinted forward, covering the lost yards at the top of the hospital corridor in a heartbeat. The head nurse never had time to look around. At full tilt, Alfred arrowed his weight at her, leading with his shoulder and barrelling her to the ground like she was one hundred years old. The chief nurse crashed sharply into the corridor wall and bounced onto the hard floor. Finally, Alfred stood over her as she softly groaned and reached for herself somehow, helpless. Alfred and Meike looked at one another.

'Let's go, Alfred,' she said.

60

'Look who I found,' Alfred announced, ushering a disbelieving Marta and Hans into the kitchen of his family home. The pair of them stepped slowly forward. It was dawn and Hans was wearing a long winter coat over pyjamas, Marta likewise over her dressing gown. Both of them only had house shoes informally on their feet. And there she was. Sat smiling at the Reis' kitchen table, hungrily eating a lashing of jam on a thick slice of fresh bread. Her features were drawn, but her essence was not now bowed. It was her. It was Meike. Marta reached up her hand to catch her mouth.

'Meike!' she cried, and a broad smile spread across Hans's face as he watched his wife rush forward and embrace their granddaughter. He stayed back and allowed the two of them to enjoy a moment.

'Hi, Grandma,' Meike said finally, almost sheepishly, as they retreated from each other briefly, Marta holding Meike by the tops of her arms and taking her in, like she needed confirmation it was really her. Everyone present, crowded into the Reis' kitchen, had been waiting to see this.

The intimate gathering included Alfred's parents, who had surprised Alfred and had revealed a side to them he could not remember, taking immediate care of Meike, making her fresh coffee, and offering her a whole week's jam ration on one, wonderful breakfast. Alfred's mother had been strict and had allowed Meike as much jam and bread as she wanted before either her husband or son could begin. They could wait.

Echoing Hans, Alfred took a step back and he looked on with a growing realisation of what he had achieved, what he had made real. *He* had done this, and if he hadn't, who knew where Meike would be right now? He tried not to recall for the moment what he had witnessed at Hadamar.

He watched Hans then finally make his way forward and hold his granddaughter lovingly. Her legs began to spasm, throwing her back with a start in the crude hospital wheelchair Alfred had exhausted himself pushing her home in through the retreating darkness. The dawning light which had accompanied them home had felt unequivocally benign, like God wanted to personally guide them home. Everyone looked worried briefly as Meike fought the spasm, but she was soon free of its judder and was able to settle people's anxious faces with smiling eyes. She was well rehearsed.

'Your medication,' Marta fussed. 'Hans! Go and get Meike's medication from home.'

'Of course,' Hans said, sharing knowing eyes with Alfred's father upon his exit.

'We've saved it all,' Marta said. 'It's all waiting for you. Come, let's get you home,' she said, half turning towards the door.

Meike looked at Alfred awkwardly. 'Thank you so much for everything,' she said out loud to the room and in the moment, Meike felt embarrassed before breaking the tension, and relishing a final, greedy bite of bread and jam, which spilled over in red ooze down her lips, which she licked. 'I'm not going home, Grandma,' she said and Marta took a step back. Silence all around. 'I'm going to be right here, Grandma,' she said, reaching out a hand and taking her grandmother's in hers. 'It will be safest. Nobody knows I'm here. I'm not going back to hospital,' she finished with a tone.

61

'We have to tell her! It's her sister,' Hans said to Marta, who was fast losing patience with him over coffee back in their own kitchen.

'The less people who know, the better, Hans,' Marta said, warming her hands protectively around her mug. 'Children like Meike were dying at that hospital, Hans… dying! What would we tell Abbe when we get him back home?'

Hans frowned, but he said nothing and turned his eyes down in quiet defeat before lifting them again.

'Those children were sick, Marta. What you're suggesting is ridiculous. We're all on the same side… we're all German. What you're saying…' But his words fell away. Marta had stopped listening.

'Oh!' she said, rising from her seat in frustration and pacing across to the kitchen sink to create what distance she could between them. Hans closed his eyes and took a breath.

'We have to tell her, Marta!' he said once more. 'She has a right to know… it's her sister, Marta.'

'God, you sound like Goebbels on the wireless each night,' Marta said, her back still to her husband under the pretence of looking out onto their back garden.

Hans scowled and tried to keep his temper as Marta hastily tossed her mug into this morning's washing water, now cold and unappealingly thin. Final dregs of coffee bloomed beneath the surface before she stopped herself. She was going to stop pretending. She was going to stop.

'I don't trust her, Hans,' she said, turning around now. 'I don't trust her.'

But Hans was rising to his feet to walk away from her. 'You have to stop this,' he said. 'I mean it, Marta… it's her sister. They're our granddaughters, they're both our granddaughters.'

Silence between the two of them, flooded with friction.

'We have to tell her,' he said again quietly.

'Tell her what?' Anselma said suddenly, appearing at the kitchen doorway.

Marta quickly turned away and plunged her hands back into their sink, washing her morning coffee mug.

'Tell her what?' Anselma said.

Don't, Marta's mind screamed at her husband. *Don't*. But…

'It's your sister, Anselma,' he said. 'She's come home.'

Marta felt herself almost drop an inch.

'Oh,' Anselma said. 'Where is she then?' she asked, and Marta could taste the sourness in her voice.

'She's staying across the street with the Reis family,' Hans said. 'For the time being… just in case the authorities want to take her back into hospital. She didn't like it… she wants to be home.' Hans tried to balance as best he could.

'Isn't hospital where she's supposed to be?' Anselma asked and Marta closed her eyes in fury.

62

Marta's eyes blinked open in darkness and focused on her bedroom ceiling. Something had disturbed her. Again. There it was. The noise which had prickled her anxiety. Car doors, multiple now, opening and closing purposefully, followed by voices, indistinct but, for the hour, urgent. Marta lay absolutely still and listened, almost not daring to move in case she somehow angered God more than she already had. *Meike*, she feared, eyes wide now with intoxication.

She scrambled out of bed and wasted valuable seconds failing to tie her dressing gown around her waist. She cursed only in her head, to avoid disturbing Hans, then she slipped her feet into her house shoes and began to pace downstairs, placing a hand to steady herself as she negotiated her way down their straight stairs. In more than one way, she knew she was uneasy.

Voices outside, louder now, more decipherable, made her skin prickle anew and she hurried her movement, dashing as fast as she could into their front room, gown billowing at bare legs. Her senses were on fire. Marta experienced her breath, in and out, in and out, as she reached their front curtains and she prepared to lift the veil on the world outside their home. She wanted to pause, she wanted to pray to God, or whoever would listen to her, but her fear was consuming and she tugged apart their thick velvet curtains and witnessed cars, unmistakeable, crowding outside the Reis' home opposite.

'Hans!' she cried.

Anselma appeared behind her, making her jump. She hadn't been able to sleep either early this morning. Marta saw she had just a nightshirt on and bare feet, a carbon copy, she knew, of her mother's, Marta's subconscious could not help but always recall with a regret.

'What is it, Grandmother?' she said.

'Where's your grandfather?' she asked impatiently.

'I think he's in bed. What is it, Grandmother?' she asked.

63

*B*ang. *Bang. Bang* on the Reis' front door. Three thuds, brutal in their brashness. Alfred jumped out of bed, wearing only pyjama bottoms, as was his habit, and stood absolutely still. *Bang, bang, bang.* A second volley at their front door, pushing him into action. He headed straight for Meike.

Alfred's mother scurried nervously down their staircase, their front door only metres in front of her. Under the pressure of the moment, she could only wrestle with the key in the lock. A third flurry of thuds, only inches from her, made her stumble back on bare heels.

'I'm here... just a moment,' she slurred, words heavy with sleep.

'Open up... open up!' a voice demanded.

'I'm here! I'm here,' she said before succeeding finally in opening their door, only to be swamped by a flood of SS and police officers pouring through her. Alfred's father appeared at the top of their stairs, wrapping a nightgown around himself, before hurrying down.

'What is the meaning of this? It is dawn, man, for God's sake!' he said.

'We're Party members.' Alfred's mother tried following the men and single woman into rooms on the ground floor of their home. 'We joined in the beginning,' she said, like it once meant something.

'Yes… yes.' A senior looking man tutted without turning around.

'Where is she?' he said bluntly, as if Alfred's mother needed reminding, and her face flushed with guilt. When she thought eyes were not on her momentarily, she blew hers up at her husband, who picked up the baton with officers.

'What is the meaning of this?' he said, approaching a bottleneck of bodies in their kitchen, which shrunk under the weight. He was surprised to see his son, Alfred, before trying to hide the emotion on his face. The lone female officer, accompanying the raid, recognised Alfred also.

'She's here,' the woman said simply to her male counterparts.

'Keep searching,' an officer said, less believing.

The officers broke up, like a flock of birds disturbed, and they searched again, with little care for the Reis' possessions and home, at one point pushing abruptly past Alfred's mother, who startled at being bumped so rudely. She stepped into a small circle of protection her husband and son had formed in their kitchen. Up close, Alfred's mother and father made eyes wider than a river at each other. They looked at their son, standing next to them, who was, for the first time in their lives, clearly taller than them both. He nodded gently and yet his parents could only frown in response, complicit in crime. To his parents, something was wrong.

Heavy steps paced the first floor of their home above them and Alfred's parents both looked up at their kitchen ceiling like they could see through it, Alfred's mother listening forensically for any clue of where the officers were searching. Alfred's eyes remained in the room. His mother gazed back down, as if she was remembering herself, and she wrapped her nightgown around her slim frame more tightly, while her son stood with pyjama bottoms below a bare chest, rippled with youth. She frowned at his state of undress. On another occasion, they would have shared happy barbs. His parents reached out and they held hands, trying to smile.

Two officers re-entered the kitchen flanked by the woman, who Alfred recognised from Hadamar, closing his eyes to her. His emotion thumped in his chest before he remembered how best to calm its beating. He couldn't concede an inch. The former head nurse of Hadamar hospital stared at Alfred, searching his face for any foothold in their search for Meike. She wanted badly to beat it out of him.

She looked down at his bare feet. Then, a rusted latch on the floor of the kitchen not far from his toes, half hidden under the table Alfred and his parents flanked. The door to a cellar. The kitchen table was hiding a door to a cellar.

64

'Look! Look, Hans!' Marta pointed with her eyeline through their living room curtains. A police officer was standing guard outside the Reis' home.

'They've come back for Meike, Hans… they've come back!' She panicked. 'We must do something… do something, Hans,' she said, turning to her husband, who was desperately processing the situation. He breathed deeply and searched within himself. He knew Marta was right and she was growing impatient.

Hans held his hands together and he looked down at them, studying the backs of them, which were like parched paper, trying to buy time, time he knew Meike perhaps didn't have. He spoke.

'We must do nothing, Marta. Otherwise, it will be clear that we know. We have to keep our heads now, as hard as it seems… for Meike.'

'For Meike!' Marta scoffed and she pulled herself away from him, freeing herself from a man who had devoted himself to her over the course of his life. Anselma timed her exit from the room, picking her way back up to her bedroom. Out of the corner of her eye, Marta was distracted, noticing her leave.

'I knew you wouldn't do anything,' Marta then said like poison and Hans almost fell back a step. Marta instantly regretted her ire, and she closed her eyes. She was infected, she knew. By her. *Her.* 'Meike needs us, Hans... we must do something!' she pleaded once more, placating her previous tone, but she had wounded him. She turned from him, and from herself.

'Stop it!' Hans said to the back of Marta's head. 'Stop it, Marta... stop.'

She turned again to face him. His dressing gown remained open from the rush of hastily hauling himself out of bed at this hour, in silk pyjama bottoms, deep claret. Marta remembered now buying them for him as a gift one Christmas. A happy day. She still wanted him.

He grabbed her arms and stepped forward into the silence which had separated them since Meike's absence. Neither had acknowledged it, but they both knew it was there, a silent wall built by divorce.

Hans's hands were strong and Marta felt them pain the inside of her wrists as he gripped them. She liked the pain now. It was a distraction. *Meike.*

Anselma.

'I'm here, Marta... I'm here,' he said, taking her eyes in his. 'I have always been here. I love that girl... I love her. You know that,' he said with an unhappiness which finally mirrored Marta's. That was all she had wanted. To know.

And there he was, standing in front of her. The man who had left her all those summers ago. July 1914. So hot she could never quite seem to catch her breath, until he had gone, forever. But now she recognised that person, that man again. She trusted him completely.

'We're praying now for Meike, Marta,' he said, sharing seamless eye contact before he closed his for a moment, like the time it took to create the stars.

Marta's face was waiting for him when he opened them.

'We'll go straight across to the Reis' house, Marta... I promise... when it is safe to do so,' he said. 'Once the police have gone. I'm going to get dressed.'

Marta watched him leave. She turned and looked through their curtains again, across the street which they had grown to know every inch of, like a lover, until the police and SS had scarred it with their presence. She witnessed the officer standing outside the Reis' home. Unmoving. *Perhaps Hans was right*, she thought, brushing her hair, tangled from sleep, with a hand off her face. She experienced a calm, as if this was the eye of a storm they had both feared and expected, and she made her way up their stairs, smoothing her hand up their banister as she did so. She enjoyed the wood's smooth sensation, seductive on her skin.

Marta reached the top of their stairs and she felt different, oddly calm. She decided to pop her head around Anselma's bedroom door and see how she was doing. This must be upsetting for her, too. Why had Marta been unable to see that before, experience that empathy for her own granddaughter? What did that make her? Anselma had lost her father and now she might lose her sister. Again. *What must I be thinking?* Marta's mind asked, approaching the door to her room. She knocked gently on it.

'Anselma?' she said, leaning her head around.

She saw her eldest granddaughter clapping her hands like a child. Not a young woman about to blossom into twenty. Marta couldn't believe what she was witnessing.

Anselma span around in her bare feet, smiling, only to be crushed by the sight of her grandmother in her doorway. Like the condemned, the happiness fell from her face.

'It was you…' Marta said, but Anselma only looked at her blankly and turned away to the window again. 'It was you,' Marta said, catching her husband's attention in the neighbouring bedroom with the sound of her tone. He stopped briefly, pulling his trousers up his legs and stood motionless, so he could listen.

Anselma looked out onto the street at the cars now leaving the Reis' home. She felt the weight of her grandmother's gaze behind her, undressing her.

65

'Gentlemen,' Devil No.2 announced. 'A door... to a cellar, beneath the table.' She pointed with her eyes and one of the men motioned forward and screeched the heavy table, roughly, to one side. Inside, Alfred's mother was dying.

'It's locked,' a man said, crouching down.

'An old wine cellar,' Alfred's father said. 'Never had any use for it. Who has wine these days?'

'The keys?' an officer said flatly, holding out a hand. 'Or you can come with us... and we won't ask politely. Keys.'

'Our housekeeper has them,' Alfred's father tried. 'She keeps the only complete set. Really... we have no use for a cellar. I have no idea what is down there, honestly.'

'The keys. Last time,' the officer said, holding his hand and failing to retreat it now. Alfred's mother stifled a sob with her hand and her husband really wished she hadn't.

'Don't worry, Father,' Alfred said, turning around to face the room. 'I know where a spare set is... in this drawer.'

His parents' faces failed to hide their quiet horror, which Devil No.2 observed with silent intoxication.

Another sob from Alfred's mother, louder now and forcing Alfred's father to hold her. The chief nurse turned to watch Alfred open a drawer and produce a rusted knot of keys. He slowly sorted through the maze of metal in his fingers before discovering the correct key and holding it up briefly to the room to communicate his success. He crouched down and he began opening the large cellar door on the floor of their kitchen, negotiating the lock, everyone's eyes heavy on him, and cranking the door open before securing it flat on the floor.

'There,' he said, standing to his feet and gesturing.

'Down,' an officer ordered, catching Alfred off guard. Alfred realised he had little choice and he gathered himself. He carefully made his way down the short ladder and was swallowed by darkness. An officer followed him, while loud calls upstairs, rehearsed, brought all of the other officers in the Reis' home downstairs to spectate. This was it, they thought.

Alfred looked down and he placed his bare feet on cold stone and the cellar floor, recently swept clean, too clean, Alfred now winced. He stood unhelping and he hid a second grimace when the officer found the switch to a light and a bulb popped, squinting into bright life above them. It revealed the space in all its plainness. An unmade bed. A bedside light. A book, thumbed. And a glass of water, half full.

'Somebody's sleeping down here,' the officer shouted above. 'And recently.'

Alfred stood to one side, unmoving. The officer took a step towards him.

'Who's living down here?' he said, and Alfred could

feel the stress in his chest as he blinked blankly back. Up close, he realised that he was taller than the man facing him. 'Who's living down here?' he asked Alfred again, and Alfred's heart beat heavy in his chest in a first flush of panic before, after a breath, he blinked blankly back.

'Up... up!' the officer sounded at Alfred, ordering him back up the ladder to the kitchen where everyone stood waiting. Alfred climbed up into the crowd of eyes and fought his fear as he got to his feet alongside everyone else. He stayed as still as possible. The chief nurse yearned to say something, but the words, like Alfred, were eluding her. What was she missing? It must be something. *It must be.*

An agony of silence. Alfred's parents eyeballed their son, what else could they do, while he willed them to look away. He cast his head slowly down.

'Take the father away,' a senior looking officer said before turning and exiting the kitchen, which prompted everyone else to follow. Hadamar's former chief nurse looked at Alfred for a time and he looked back. How the devil in him wanted to smile. *Not now, Alfred.* Nearly home. *Eight, nine, ten. Then chaos.*

The former chief nurse was about to shake her head before she turned her back on Alfred and his parents and walked out of their kitchen, the last to leave, which signalled Mr and Mrs Reis to soon collapse in relief and gasp for air like they had been submerged under water. Alfred continued to quietly hold his breath. On the other side of their pantry door, neighbouring the Reis' kitchen, Meike heard footsteps leaving the kitchen and she began to dare let out a breath she had been burying inside her for what felt like her whole life following her accident. First, it slowly filled her lungs before shifting benignly up her breast and finally her throat, releasing from her mouth.

As Meike had held her breath through the search of the Reis' home, her imagination had pictured a memory of her father, stroking gently the hair from her eyebrows and smiling at her as she sat in her chair looking back at him, in his study at their now empty family home in the country lanes bordering Berlin. Together, like seasoned spies, they had been secretly listening to the BBC World Service on Abbe's longwave radio. Nobody else knew that they were and that by doing so they were risking breaking new laws. Meike cherished the clandestine moment with an ache of her heart.

In her imagination, she had watched him dismantle the radio in two, hiding one half in a box, on a shelf in the corner of his study, meantime, placing the other quite unprotected on an opposite shelf in broad view of anyone entering the room. The policy happily puzzled Meike, sat watching. She was curious. What was her father thinking?

'Hide in plain sight, Meike,' he said to her, timeless in the memory. 'People so often miss what is right in front of them,' he said, tapping a comic finger in the air in exclamation. 'Very often, my darling, don't look beyond it in search of something that was never there,' he said as Meike took a thousand images in her mind.

The door to the Reis' pantry then opened before her and Meike blinked, and she saw Alfred and his mother looking at her. She paused before smiling and pushing in her chair back into the kitchen. Empty once more. And safe, she was safe.

Alfred pulled the kitchen table back carefully over

the cellar door, tidying the space so it was just how his mother liked it and erasing, for now, thoughts of who had just been here. Once Alfred had finished doing so, Meike collapsed her hands and arms, and the top of her chest, onto the table and almost hugged it.

'Clever boy, Alfred,' his mother said, clasping the tops of his arms and looking at him and Meike as if they were one now. 'Clever boy.'

Alfred smiled quietly back and looked at Meike for what felt like a long time. Marta then burst into the space and wrapped herself around her youngest granddaughter like she would never let go.

'Meike!' she cried. 'Meike,' she said softly, cupping her face like a jewel.

'I'm okay, Grandma,' she said, freeing herself from her embrace slightly. Marta wiped away tears and she caught Alfred's mother's eye and together, they shared a warm smile. 'Hans has followed the police to find out where they are taking Mr Reis. We'll find him. We'll get him back,' Marta said, swallowing a lack of confidence.

'I'm going to get dressed,' Alfred said and everyone was grateful for the notion of the everyday. He rose from his seat and looked again at Meike.

'I'll put a pot of coffee on,' Alfred's mother said, picking up on her son's sentiment. 'Fresh.'

Marta smiled and took a seat at the table next to Meike. They held each other's hands.

66

Twenty-Five Years Later

'That was delicious,' said Alfred, looking across their modest dining table at Meike. 'That steak… I'll never be able to order it in a restaurant again!'

This made Meike, with the back of her hand to her forehead, feign comic modesty. Alfred smiled widely and felt a rush of happiness. Life, simply, with her was luxury.

He rose from his seat and began tidying their supper plates away before carrying them the short distance to their adjoining kitchen in the open, ground floor apartment, small to grandiose eyes, but perfect for them. They had an unspoken agreement: Meike cooked, Alfred washed up. They both knew it was a good trade.

Alfred began filling their sink with soapy water as Meike pushed in her chair behind him to their fridge, opening the door and reaching for a bottle of wine she never quite made last a whole week. She poured herself the thin side of half a glass and she wheeled over to Alfred to embrace the back of his waist.

A knock at the door. Strange. *Our guest this evening is early*, thought Meike, turning her head to take in the clock on their wall. *That's not like her.* Alfred half turned and saw Meike begin pushing to their front door before casually returning his attention to washing their supper plates. At their front door, Meike strained to reach up and unlock the latch, and open their door. She did so and then blinked in shock.

'Anselma,' she said, looking up.

'Meike.'

For the next moment, neither of them said anything.

'Would you like to come in?' Meike said, breaking the silence and feeling she had little choice. She span around in her chair, anticipating her sister would accept her invitation and follow her in.

'Yes… please,' said Anselma, stepping into the light of their home.

As she began walking through her sister's apartment, her mind could not help judging it. At the end of the short entrance hallway, she flashed past a mirror and eyed herself sideways as, ahead, Meike pushed into the apartment's main space. She was trying not to think too hard.

Anselma removed her coat and handed it to her sister like it was more expensive than it looked. Alfred was poised to make a joke before hastily retreating from the thought and instead, letting his face fall flat too quickly.

'Anselma,' he said.

'Alfred,' said Anselma, taking his usual seat at their dining table without invitation.

'Would you like a drink, Anselma?' Meike said, finding

it strange, in the moment, to say her sister's name out loud. 'Coffee?'

'Do you have wine?' she said.

Meike poured her the last glass from the bottle, which Anselma proceeded to drink too quickly, Meike noticed with a secret roll of an eye. She had never known Anselma to drink like that before.

'I guess you're wondering why I'm here,' she said, looking down, eyes fixed on the last of the wine in her glass.

'No,' Meike said. 'Yes,' she then said, deciding quickly to drop the pretence and pushing over to accompany her at their table while, in the background, Alfred continued to clean their supper dishes at their sink.

Anselma looked over her sister at Alfred and then leant into Meike. 'Could we speak, somewhere…?'

Meike looked over her shoulder momentarily. 'It's fine, Anselma. We can speak here.'

Anselma rolled her eyes and then immediately regretted doing so. *Why did she always feel like this?* In one mouthful, she finished the last of her wine.

'I want a divorce from Reinhold. I need money,' she said. 'I can pay you back from the settlement… once it is through. I will do very well,' she said instinctively, picturing her husband, who she hated more than Jews. Silence as Meike considered how to answer, Alfred quietening what he was doing to a hush.

Anselma watched her sibling wrestling with her conscience.

'Failure is like a disease, Meike,' Anselma said, almost looking up and continuing to hold her empty wine glass with both her hands. 'It passes from one generation to the next. If I had only known...' She began to laugh uncomfortably. 'I need money, Meike,' she said, and trying now to make eye contact as Meike continued to think, finding it simpler to focus on Anselma's empty glass sat between them on the otherwise cleared table, which separated them like Berlin's new wall.

'We haven't got anything, Anselma,' she said before her sister quickly spoke.

'Life has always been easy for you, Meike,' she said. 'I know I wasn't very kind...'

Nothing for a moment as Meike protected herself and pretended she had not heard the confession, which carried a lifetime of emotion.

'You should go,' said Meike. 'We have a friend coming.'

Anselma sniffed and nodded, lifting herself from the seat at their table and looking down briefly at her worn shoes she wished she could replace. She raised her eyes and looked up. She saw Alfred standing protectively over her sister. Her eyes were drawn to their fingers reaching for each other's.

Alfred handed Anselma her coat and he closed the front door behind his sister-in-law without any more words between them. He turned around and smiled softly at Meike before a knock at their door made him jump. Meike giggled, making him laugh at himself. He turned around again and opened the door to their apartment and a woman, almost as tall as Alfred, stood, beaming in their doorway. Her face flooded the entrance to their home like the morning sun.

'Alfred!' she said quietly, as only she could, throwing herself at him in a hug.

'Meike.' She smiled, looking over Alfred's shoulder and untying herself from him, walking over to where her friend of all these years was. The woman bent down and the two of them embraced. Meike squeezed her friend from Hadamar. The woman who still looked like a boy came around most evenings after dinner for dessert.